Us & Them

by Hugh R. MacDonald

Praise for *Trapper Boy*
by Hugh R. MacDonald

"Excellent literature and ought to win prizes. Highly Recommended." *CM* Magazine

Mr. MacDonald makes conditions and routine in the mine so vivid…. The language is plain, but correct." Charlottetown *Guardian*

This is an especially compelling story that middle school students will relate to and enjoy.
Resources for Thinking

"A wonderful piece of storytelling ... it's not only a good story, it's a history of coal mining in Cape Breton ... a heartbreaking and emotional account.... It's the kind of book that should be used for history classes in high school and universities." Sheldon Currie

Teachers!
There is a free teacher resource available for Hugh R. MacDonald's *Trapper Boy*. It was prepared for CBU Press by Patrick Howard, Department of Education,Cape Breton University
Free download: http://tinyurl.com/zadxpzn
(http://cbup.ca/wp/wp-content/Special/Trapper-Boy-Teacher-Resource.pdf)

To my wife, Joanne,
and to the memory of our beloved son, Keith,
and our coal-mining grandfathers,
Red Jack MacDonald and Charles Dawe.

Cover image: Princess Colliery at Sydney Mines, 1916.
      80-31-4211. Beaton Institute, Cape Breton University.
Cover design: Cathy MacLean Design, Chéticamp, NS
Author photo: Michael G. MacDonald
Layout: Mike Hunter, West Bay and Sydney, NS
Edited by Marianne Ward, Dartmouth, NS

First printed in Canada

Library and Archives Canada Cataloguing in Publication
MacDonald, Hugh R., 1956-, author
      Us and them : a novel / Hugh R. MacDonald.

Issued in print and electronic formats.
ISBN 978-1-77206-065-2 (paperback).--ISBN 978-1-77206-066-9 (pdf).
ISBN 978-1-77206-067-6 (epub).--ISBN 978-1-77206-068-3 (kindle)
      I. Title.
PS8625.D637U72 2016   jC813'.6   C2016-905077-7
                                                   C2016-905078-5

RECYCLED
Paper made from
recycled material
FSC
www.fsc.org   FSC® C103567

Cape Breton University Press   Sold and Distributed by
PO Box 5300   Nimbus Publishing
Sydney, Nova Scotia B1P 6L2 Canada   3731 MacKintosh St
                                       Halifax, Nova Scotia B3K 5A5 Canada

www.cbupress.ca

                                       www.nimbus.ca

Us & Them

by Hugh R. MacDonald

Cape Breton University Press
Sydney, Nova Scotia, Canada

Us & Them

Chapter 1

JW awoke and sat up in bed. The dream was so vivid. Red, the boss, and some faceless men were taking him from the mine, telling him that it was too late and that nothing could be done. He heard tapping coming from the other side of the tunnel; it became fainter as he was led to the surface. He always woke at this point, never knowing if the others in the dream got out. In reality he had played a role in the outcome so he knew what happened, but he wondered how the dream version would end if he stayed sleeping.

"John Wallace," his mother called. She was the only person who called him by his full name anymore. Even his high school teachers called him JW. "It's almost seven o'clock, and I expect your father along soon."

It was JW's job to get the eggs and milk in the morning. He usually got the coal and wood in the night before.

"Be right there, Ma." He pulled on his clothes and hurried down the stairs. As a boy, JW's favourite breakfast meal had always been porridge, but now, at sixteen, he had grown to like eggs and was glad they had lots of chickens. Their goat had gotten ill and died and had been replaced by a cow. It had taken a little while to get used to milking the cow, but there was so much more milk that they could now have butter and cheese in abundance.

With his father working full-time hours now as an overman, having replaced Red as boss, they had the money to plant bigger gardens, as well as a field of hay. The harvest was a lot of work, but it enabled them to keep the cow. Their horse, Lightning, was getting old, but was busy during hay-making time and didn't appear any worse for wear, despite his age. JW was kept busy with his chores, but during the summer he had lots of time for fishing and swimming.

His family was lucky to have inherited Grandfather Donaldson's farm. Situated on the outskirts of town, the property had lots of fields to roam. It was a mile-and-a-half walk to school each day, but at the midway point JW met up with his girlfriend, Beth Jessome, which made the rest of the walk more enjoyable. Her family owned a small two-acre farm, which gave them enough land to plant a garden and keep a goat for milk. Her father worked away, leaving the chores to Beth, her sister and mother.

JW's father, Andrew, worked in the coal mine near town. Most of the men in the area did. In fact, a number of JW's friends worked in the coal mines and lived in the company houses. His best friend, Mickey, was one of them. After completing grade six, he had gone to work there first on the surface at the breakers, picking rocks and shale from the coal, and then underground as a trapper boy. At barely twelve years of age, Mickey had gone into the mine as a trapper boy, opening and closing the door that kept the fresh air deep in the mines. JW had followed him two years later and had worked long enough to know it was not a life he'd choose. But hard times meant lots of young boys continued to work there, including Mickey. JW was glad he'd been able to leave.

He'd grown over the past three winters, and JW was now taller than his father. He'd heard his mother tell his father he was big for his age, and his father had laughed, saying he was big for any age. Many of the tunnels where his father and others worked were only three or four feet high, some even less. JW figured that by now he'd be bent in half in some of them.

He knew that by his age most of the boys in the mine would no longer be on the trap doors. They would be using picks and shovels like the other men, or leading horses, pulling coal-filled trams throughout the mine. Mickey had told JW that he was hoping to move off the trap door soon, maybe go shovelling coal and eventually move to what JW's father had done, room and pillar mining. That job scared JW. It included using a pick to pull down the tunnel ceiling once the room had been mined for coal – it was known as the miner's harvest. He remembered what his father had said when he'd asked him why the men would take such a chance.

"The coal is right above you for the taking. There's tons of it. It's a chance for the men to make a decent day's pay. You just got to keep your mind on the task at hand, and when you hear it getting ready to let go, run like the devil."

It was only the skill of the miner that prevented injury – or worse.

JW's experience with a pick and shovel had improved, although not from work in the coal mines. The irrigation trenches he'd dug last summer had taught him how to make the pick do the work. He figured it was different than with coal but didn't want to find out for sure. Still, there had been a lot of stone and rocks he'd had to dig through. Shovelling the earth from the trenches had helped him build muscle. With his father so busy at the mine, JW expected that he would cut the wood this year all by himself too. The days were getting longer, and there was only a month left of school; 1929 was almost half over, and JW was looking forward to the coming summer. He hoped to start on the wood soon.

JW placed the basket filled with eggs on the kitchen table. There were close to twenty in it.

"Oh dear, I'll have to do some baking to use up the eggs. There are already more than a dozen in the icebox. Take six or so with you to Beth's mother, will you please?" his mother said.

"Sure. I still have to get the milk," JW said, and picked up the bucket. The cow stood unmoving, munching on some hay, but it still took some time to finish the milking. JW was glad his father had put in the icebox. Storing the milk and other perishable goods in the well had worked okay, but the icebox kept things fresher much longer. His parents shared any surplus food with others.

Breathing in the odours of musty hay and manure, JW looked around the barn. He noted the various objects that hung from the rafters: saddles, bridles and reins, and there was a rusty old scythe used to cut hay. He was glad to have the hay cutter that he could sit on as Lightning pulled it through the fields. JW couldn't imagine having to try to cut all that hay with a scythe. Still, he'd rather cut hay with a scythe than work underground again.

Because he had worked nights in the mine, he'd tried going to school during the days and sleeping in the afternoons but only managed to do it for a short time before he had to quit. When his father took a better paying job, JW returned to grade nine. With Beth's help and that of his teachers – Mr. Cantwell and Mrs. Johnson – he had managed to finish better than the middle of the pack for grade nine. Without having to work in the mine, grade ten had seen him return to being a top student, and this year in grade eleven he continued to excel.

When he was younger, he enjoyed getting lost in his books of adventure, but his time in the coal mine had made him curious about the world in a different way. He wondered how many other children worked in dangerous conditions. He had asked the librarian to keep an eye out for any books on the topic. It had taken some time, but he'd just gotten a book written by John Spargo, *The Bitter Cry of the Children*. Mrs. Johnson said he could keep it for as long as he needed. He planned to read it to learn what other children had had to endure. Long Jack, who'd been injured in the coal mine, once told him that years ago girls as young as five and six used to work the trap doors in Scotland, England and Wales. Long Jack operated the streetcar that ran between Sydney Mines and North Sydney but said he hoped to get back underground soon.

Long Jack said his grandpa had come from Scotland and had told him the girls and women had been badly treated. He'd said that anytime laws were changed to try to make better working conditions, the owners just agreed to change but didn't until forced to many years later. JW had been afraid working underground, and he'd been thirteen. *It must have been so much worse for those little girls,* he thought. He wondered what had happened to the culture of knights and chivalry. Perhaps it only existed in books.

Chapter 2

JW came out of the barn in time to see his dog, Gulliver, running to meet his father. He watched his father reach to pet him. Gulliver's head and tail shook, and the rest of him went into a full-body shuffle. It was Gulliver's way of letting you know he was happy to see you.

"How'd it go last night, Da? Still having trouble with the new tunnel?"

"Yeah, the water's still coming in. Pretty soon I expect some fish."

JW laughed, thinking of the stories his father used to tell. While he no longer sat at the table in anticipation of adventures in the mine, JW liked to hear of the challenges the men faced.

"Oh yeah," his father said. "Mick asked if you could meet him Saturday to do a little fishing."

"Tell him I can, unless you got some chores that can't wait, that is," JW said.

"I'm sure they can wait."

"Tell him we can meet at the old fort, or he can come here. Maybe catch a few trout, then try for some codfish later on," JW said. He lifted the bucket high enough to keep Gulliver's nose from dipping into it. His father opened the back door, and they went in for breakfast. JW watched as his mother added some milk and onions to the eggs before putting them into the hot pan. The eggs fluffed up and turned a golden brown – soon they were done. JW piled lots on his plate.

He listened to his parents talk and nodded when included in the conversation. They laughed and talked about work and school and things that needed to be done, but JW knew there were lots of homes in the area where parents were making tough decisions; boys his age and younger were being told they'd be heading to work in the coal mines.

JW drank the last of his tea, thanked his mother and got up from the table. He placed his dishes in the sink before he picked up his satchel and the eggs and headed for the door. "Da, I cleaned the stalls, and I'll get in the coal and kindling after school. See you later."

"Okay, I'll leave them be," his father said.

"Only seems fair. You're the working man these days," JW said, and they all laughed. During the months JW had spent underground, two and a half years earlier, his father had tried his best to help by doing most of the chores that JW had usually done. His parents were still laughing at his comment as he closed the kitchen door behind him.

"You know, Mary," Andrew said, as JW left for school, "it's hard watching the young boys that continue to come underground. Mickey's been down there almost four years, and Patty close to three. I wish things would pick up so that no more children end up there."

"I know, Andrew, dear, but you got JW out, and you treat the other boys well, so at least that's something."

"Yeah, I guess it's something. Young Mick has asked about moving off the trap to go shovelling coal. He said he wants to do what I used to do. I felt a shiver at the thought of him doing that. Could be JW." Andrew felt the strong hand of his wife on his arm.

"But it's not. And you'll make sure Mickey's well trained before you let him—"

"That's just it. I've no time to watch out for them like I want to. Mick should do alright, but I'd like to keep young Patty on the trap for a while longer. But the way he follows Mickey around when they're on the same shift, I'm sure he'll want to move on too – ready or not."

"Best get to bed, dear. Try to get some rest."

Mary watched as Andrew walked to their bedroom. She knew if JW was here, he'd surely notice the deep creases in his father's face.

"C'mon, Gullie, I have to go to school. Walk me to Beth's," JW said, and knelt to hug his faithful dog.

JW felt the wind picking up as he reached the hill above Beth's house. Gulliver's wagging tail tapped against JW's leg as he waited to be petted.

"Good boy, Gullie. Run on home," JW said. He gave him a pat then watched as Gullie trotted back the way they'd come.

A few drops of rain landed on the satchel he used to carry his books and lunch. JW hoped they wouldn't get a shower before he and Beth got to school. He wiped the rain from the satchel. His grandfather, Wallace Donaldson, had made it for him when JW was five. Grandpa Donaldson had told him it would last a lifetime, and JW believed it would. He walked quickly down the hill and arrived at Beth's door just as she was coming out.

"Ma sent these for your mother," JW said, holding out the eggs.

Beth took them inside and returned quickly. "Ma said to tell her thanks. You're here early today. Trouble sleeping?"

"Not really, but I had that dream again. The cave-in. You know."

"Yeah," Beth said, and shuddered.

"Oh, Da said Mickey wants to go fishing on Saturday, and I said I'd go." As soon as the words left his mouth, he remembered he was supposed to spend the day with Beth at the fort he and Mickey had built by their swimming hole. Beth had helped fix it up, and they used it to change into their swimming clothes. There were times when Mickey would get close to a week off at a time during the summer if the mine shut down.

"I'm sorry, Beth. I forgot about our date to go to the fort for a picnic, and I know we were going to do some studying and reading. I'll tell Da to tell Mickey I can't make it this weekend."

"Don't be silly. Ma will find lots for me to do. Poor Mickey doesn't get to do much fishing."

"You can come too," JW said, but he knew fishing with him and Mickey wasn't her idea of fun. Beth liked Mickey, but when JW and Mickey got together they engaged in a little too much tomfoolery for her liking. Beth was becoming quite a young lady, and her tomboy behaviour was in the past.

"No, we'll just meet tonight to study, and you go with Mickey tomorrow."

"Yeah, exams aren't far off, so I guess we should. Do you want to come to my place, or should we meet at yours?" JW carried her books and felt her arm go around his waist as they walked toward school. His satchel tapped lightly against his leg.

"Ma wants me to help with some baking after school, so you might as well come over. You can do some taste testing."

JW smiled. He loved to have a second dessert. "Okay, I'll come over around six o'clock. That way I'll have time to get my chores done."

Beth gave JW's hand an extra squeeze, then let it go as the school came into view. "See you after school," Beth said, and walked over to meet her friends.

Chapter 3

Lightning moved aside as JW entered the stall, making the soft whinny of familiarity. JW held the oats in his hand, waiting as Lightning ate slowly, savouring the grain. JW had learned that if he wasn't going to exercise Lightning, he had to reduce the amount of oats he gave him. His father had told him that too much oats made horses excitable, and they needed to run or work it off. JW felt bad cutting back on the oats, so he generally added extra hay.

"You'll get lots of oats soon, old boy, once we start the planting. You'll need all the energy you can get to dig up those old fields – all you can eat then," JW said, as he began to brush him down.

He wondered what his father would think if he knew he'd been riding on Lightning's back. He hadn't broken him to a saddle but, after being thrown to the ground a few times, he had been able to convince Lightning to allow him to ride on his back. JW remembered lying on the ground the first time after being thrown, the wind knocked out of him. He cleaned the rest of the stall and walked toward the door.

JW noticed Tennyson, his pet rat, sitting on the small woodpile that remained stacked in the barn. He was getting pretty old and no longer ventured outside. His girlfriend, as JW's father had called her, had been picked off by a small hawk, but Tennyson, bad leg and all, had made it back inside the barn. His was now a solitary life. JW noticed there was a lot of grey in Tennyson's whiskers and facial hair, making him wonder what the life span of a rat actually was. He grabbed some oats and laid them on the wood beside Tennyson. "Eat up, old boy," JW said. He suddenly realized that he referred to Gulliver, Lightning and Tennyson all as "old boy" quite often when he spoke to them. Gulliver and Tennyson had not become friends, but they tolerated each other.

Tennyson was a constant reminder of the time JW had spent in the mine. As a young rat in search of food underground, he had run up JW's pant leg. Startled, JW had gotten hold of his tail and flung the rat against the wall, injuring his leg. Feeling guilty, he later smuggled Tennyson – named for one of JW's favourite poets – out of the mine, concealed in his satchel. He wasn't sure what others would think of him taking a rat home.

JW heard Gulliver bark and went outside. Mickey was coming toward him. His friend had grown tall over the past two years, but JW was a few inches taller. Their friend Patty hadn't seemed to grow much at all. He was usually working the opposite shift to Mickey, so the three seldom got together. What Mickey lacked in height, he made up for in width. Although he was still working at the trap door, Mickey hauled coal with his father on his days off, which accounted for the extra muscle. Mickey had told JW that he and his father were partners in the coal hauling business.

"I do all the work, and Da gets all the money," Mickey had said jokingly, but JW believed it was probably close to the truth. Mickey's father, Shawn McGuire, was mean-tempered much of the time.

"Hey, JW. Ready to go?"

"Yep. Chores are all done, and my lunch is packed," JW answered.

"That all you think about – food?" Mickey asked.

"Yep. Doesn't look like you miss too many meals, either." Holding up the satchel, JW said, "I was at Beth's last night. I've got some cake and cookies in here, enough for the two of us."

Mickey smiled. "I figured we'd catch some fish for lunch, but cake and cookies sound like a good backup." Gulliver bounded alongside the two boys as they headed for the riverbank. As they'd grown older, they'd realized what they'd called a river was really only a brook, but they still called the side of the brook the riverbank.

Neither seemed to want to break the early morning silence as they walked along. Only the crunching of stones underfoot disturbed the quiet. Gulliver moved from JW to Mickey in his quest to be petted.

—

Beth looked around the Co-operative store. There was everything in here that she could possibly need or want. Her parents, like JW's, didn't have a lot of extra money, but still she liked to spend time gazing at all the goods that were housed under the Co-operative's roof. Her mother hadn't needed anything today, but since JW was off fishing with Mickey, Beth had decided to walk to town once her chores had been completed – just to look around. Beth's father was a carpenter and spent months away at a time, working and learning new skills in Louisbourg, which was on the other side of the Island. Her mother, besides raising Beth and her younger sister, was a seamstress, making beautiful clothes for those who could afford them.

"Surprised to see you in town today, with a big test coming on Monday."

Beth turned to face Davey Brown. "I guess I could say the same of you," Beth said.

"True, but I live in town," Davey said.

"Well, JW and I studied last evening, and we'll go over it again later tonight."

"It's a good thing he's got you to help him," Davey said.

"Oh, he doesn't need my help. We help each other," Beth said.

"Where is he today? Working on the farm?" Davey asked. There was more than a hint of disdain in his tone.

"No, he's fishing with his friend Mickey."

"I'd never leave a pretty girl like you alone to go off fishing with a friend," Davey said. He turned quickly and left the store. The bell above the door clanged loudly.

Beth blushed at his words and watched as Davey hurried up the street without a backward glance.

"I think he's sweet on you, Beth," Mrs. Ferneyhough said, then added, "Anything I can get you, dear?"

Beth blushed a deeper red when she saw that Mr. Ferneyhough was smiling. "No thank you, Mrs. Ferneyhough," she said, and left the store. She remembered JW's mother had said the same words to her two years earlier about JW, *I think he's sweet on you, dear*. Beth wondered what had gotten into Davey. He was aware that she and JW were boyfriend and girlfriend. She pushed the thought to the back of her mind.

Chapter 4

"And then Mickey fell backwards into the pool, and I couldn't get a good grip on him 'cause of all the mud, and he had to walk downstream...."

Beth heard JW's voice, but she was thinking of her trip to town and not really paying attention to what he was saying. She didn't know whether or not she should tell JW about Davey.

"We got trout and codfish too. I brought some for your mother," JW said, and handed the fish to her.

"Thanks. I'll give these to Ma later." Beth sighed. "I was in town today, and I saw Davey Brown. Out of the blue, he said he wouldn't leave a pretty girl like me alone to go fishing with a friend. I don't mean that I'm pretty. I just thought I should tell you what he said."

"Oh, he got that part right. You're the prettiest girl in town. The prettiest in the whole world," JW said, and then blushed. "You know what I mean. He can think all he wants, but I'm gonna have a talk with him. Set him straight."

They'd gotten together to study for the evening, but JW spent much of the time glancing over at Beth.

"Well that's as much as I can do tonight," Beth said, pushing the books to the middle of the table.

"Me too. Is there time to go for a little walk?"

"Sure. You can help me put some feed out for the animals."

The chickens squawked as JW and Beth entered the barn. With Beth's father away in Louisbourg, the Jessomes had had to sell their cow; it was too much work for Beth and her mother. They still had a goat – one of the kids that JW's goat had given birth to. It was full-grown now and provided them with enough milk to cover their needs. JW brought cheese and butter over from time to time as well as eggs, because the Jessomes' two hens didn't account for many eggs in the run of a week. They were very proud people, like his own family, and Mrs. Jessome, in return, sent fancy lace doilies to JW's mother. They were made from the end pieces left over from material used to make curtains and other articles for the town's more affluent citizens. This exchange meant JW's mother had pretty decorations she could never afford, and Beth's mother got what she needed without having to spend her meagre earnings on necessities.

JW believed this sort of exchange, the barter system or sharing of surplus goods, was what established a true sense of community. He had been thinking a lot about that sort of thing recently. After entering the mine as a trapper boy, JW had attended a union meeting with his father and heard a speech by JB McLachlan. James Bryson McLachlan was a union organizer and advocate for miners' rights. JW had subsequently gotten to know JB, who espoused communal ownership as a preferred economic system.

JW understood the attractiveness of such a system, especially among the poor and destitute. Everyone got an equal share, at least in theory. But after thinking about it for a while, JW wasn't convinced it was best. Perhaps parts of the communal system could be used to improve the present one that left miners and their families to live in poverty. Sadly, profit over people seemed to be what best suited the mine owners, as JB was quick to point out. JW liked McLachlan and hoped to spend more time learning from him. JB had become a local legend. He had gone to jail for speaking out against management practices at the mine and for encouraging civil disobedience.

JW watched as Beth swept a wisp of hair away from her face. He put his hand on her shoulder.

"Are you upset I went fishing with Mickey?"

"Of course not. I mean I was a little surprised that you'd forgotten we were going to spend the day together. But I wasn't angry. Besides, we have the whole summer to go to the fort."

JW felt Beth move into his arms and was relieved. He kissed her and then held her tightly. He knew how he felt about her, but perhaps he didn't tell her enough. "You know you're the only girl for me, don't you?"

Beth moved backwards and looked up at him. She smiled. "Yes, I do, and I told you before, you're the only boy for me, JW, which is why I told you what Davey said. We better get back in. I have to get up early for church."

"I better get on home too. See you at church," JW said, and kissed her again. He didn't want to leave her. Perhaps he had been taking Beth for granted, and Davey thought he spotted an opening to move in. Davey Brown's family had lots of money, and his father was JW's father's boss. There were a lot of advantages for Beth to be involved with Davey, but she'd just told him that he was the only boy for her. Still, he worried. He'd make plans to take her to the theatre to see a matinee soon.

When he got to the top of the hill he turned back to look at Beth's house. He could make out her silhouette in the darkness. He waved and thought he saw her return the gesture. He'd always thought he was in no hurry to be a grownup because of the extra worry grown-ups had. But he'd seen how his relationship with Beth had changed in the past year.

"Guess it's time to grow up," he said aloud, and jumped a little when Gulliver's wet nose tapped his fingers. He hadn't been paying attention but was glad his old friend had come to walk him home. He petted his head and rubbed his shoulders. The time spent in the pit had pretty much cured JW of his fear of the dark, but he still liked that Gulliver came to meet him when the long shadows made the tree limbs look like arms reaching toward him. That he no longer had to pass the graveyard late at night on the way to the mine was something he didn't mind either.

Chapter 5

JW's mind drifted back to the afternoon spent with Mickey, thinking he might not be able to take too many more of those for a while.

There was Mickey, covered in mud. JW couldn't help laughing. He'd watched as one of Mickey's feet had slipped over the side of the bank. Swinging his arms wildly, he had almost regained his balance before falling backward into the stream. They'd sat around the fire, cooking the trout they'd caught, waiting for Mickey's clothes to dry.

"So how are things at the trap?"

"Not much change there, JW. You know. Nice guys like Smitty and then there are guys like Old Man Reilly, and Da's no better. They both still pick on poor Patty when your father's not around. I don't think he's grown an inch since you had him in that headlock. I think you stunted his growth. When I say I'm going to move to shovelling coal, he says he's gonna follow me. He's strong for his size, but I don't think he'd be able to keep up. Maybe he could go on a scale job weighing coal or, I dunno, something else. I feel like I gotta look out for him."

JW remembered the first night Patty had started in the pit and the fight between them. JW was on the winning side. Now, he watched the turmoil in Mickey's face and wished he could suggest something to help Patty. "Maybe he'd be good at the start of a new tunnel. You know, getting in the small places."

"Yeah, but that's where the blasting happens, and some of the experienced men get hurt on those jobs. It's like, I want him on the surface where it's safer, but those are the jobs for the older guys. Some of them, I should say. There are some older men missing body parts who are still working underground."

JW looked at Mickey and realized he was being serious. *What choice do the men have?* he thought. If your family's hungry, you have to work. "Guess that's what JB McLachlan was talking about when he was trying to rally the men. The rights of the workers. Too sick or too old to work. There ought to be something – some kind of fund to look after them."

"That stint in jail sure knocked ol' JB for a loop," Mickey said. "You're right though, there should be something for the folks when they're old or sick. But who can save anything when you don't make enough to live on to start with? Maybe it'll get better."

JW picked up a rock and tossed it to Mickey. "Remember the night we went looking for the fossils, and I asked you to walk me back to the trap door? I didn't want to tell you I was scared, so I let on I was worried the door wouldn't open. Did you ever find anymore fossils?"

"I remember. I was just as afraid as you – just more used to the walk. But no, I never went looking after that night, and since I was in the cave-in I stay pretty close to the trap door." They looked at each other, remembering that night, the one JW relived in his dreams. "Don't want to end up trapped again without you there to help dig us out," Mickey said, half joking, half serious.

"I know we don't talk about it much," he continued, "but tell me about the cave-in, right from the start."

It was a night neither JW nor Mickey would ever forget – nor would their families.

"Ma tried to hide the scared look on her face when she told me about the cave-in," JW said. "Her words played over and over in my mind as I ran toward the mine. My satchel was banging off my leg."

"What'd she say to ya?" Mickey asked.

"Her exact words were, 'John Wallace! Get up, dear! There's been a cave-in at the mine. You have to go help. Hurry along. There's men trapped.'"

"That musta scared ya."

"Sure did. When I got to the mine and heard someone tell Red that six men were trapped with little chance of being rescued, I was pretty scared. Then when I heard it was Da, you and Smitty trapped, I knew I had to try something. One of the rescue guys said the roof let go and a couple of the timbers cracked and that there was close to a hundred ton of coal in the tunnel."

Mickey nodded his head for JW to go on.

"When the man told Red that the air in there wouldn't last long, I hurried down to where you were trapped. If it hadn't been for Da drawing me pictures of the underground workings of the mine, I wouldn't have known where to start. It was like I had a map or something. I went in the old worked-out tunnel where you and I had gone looking for fossils, 'cause that's where the tunnels converged."

"I heard the tapping noise coming through to us," Mickey said, "and I saw your father stand right up and start swinging his pick to match whoever was on the other side. Da held back. He seemed more scared than anyone. I was embarrassed when he was the first one through the hole ya dug for us."

"It was kinda strange seeing him scurrying from the hole first."

"Don't think he'll ever live that down. Miners have long memories," Mickey said.

"Da said Grandpa had an old saying that 'it's an ill wind that blows no good,'" JW said.

"Ma says that too. Living with the old fella, she's seen a lot of ill winds – not many good ones," Mickey said.

"Being trapped in the cave-in must have been terrifying for all of you, just lucky no one was hurt. If it hadn't happened, I'd probably still be working there. Remember Red showed up with Mr. Brown, the mine manager?"

"Not really, I just remember Red leading us out of there to the surface," Mickey said. "What about it?"

"I heard Mr. Brown tell another man that there was no one to replace Red. I told him Da could do the job because he knew how everything worked underground. At first he didn't want to listen, but when I pulled Da's sketches from my satchel and showed him the same pictures I'd used to find you, he paid more attention and eventually hired Da to be the new boss."

"I don't want to be part of these kinds of stories any-more. Now I stay pretty close to the trap door. Like I said, I don't want to get trapped unless you're there to dig us out."

"Don't get trapped then, 'cause I don't plan on going back in," JW said, and laughed.

"Not if I can help it, anyway. Still have plans to sail the seven seas. Beth's pa's been working on a schooner in Louis-bourg and was telling me about it."

JW laughed again, this time at himself. "Been talking to Smitty about Barbados, and he says he's all set to go back as soon as I have my own schooner ready." Smitty was the first man to take the time to stop and talk to JW when he was working the trap door. Both of Smitty's parents were teach-ers, and JW figured he was as smart as they come. "He told me about the white sands of Barbados and how he'd love to return home one day," JW continued. "I told him it might be a while yet."

"Don't forget I'm going as first mate. Or deckhand. I don't care as long as I'm on board."

"Lots of room on the raft. Even has a sail on it."

They laughed and got ready to go fishing codfish, now that Mickey's clothes had dried and the trout were eaten. They threw some dirt on the remaining embers of the fire and headed for their favourite spot on Bras d'Or Lake – the Rock, a group of shale rocks that jutted out into the water.

As they crossed the train tracks and started down the embankment to St. Andrew's Channel, JW glanced ahead to the beach where they had left their raft. It was now leaning up against a large stone. The small piece of canvas that was their sail covered the gap between raft and rock, like a lean-to. JW marvelled that the wind and tide could have thrown it that way, but as they made their way down the bank, someone came out from under the sail and hurried down the shore, away from them. JW noticed the man walked with a limp, his sturdy stick seemed to propel him down the beach. A small pack was slung over his shoulder. JW called after the man, but he did not stop or turn around.

Chapter 6

JW and Mickey had split the cod they'd caught between them, and JW knew it would be appreciated by both of their mothers. He had more than they could eat in a week. JW was glad he'd taken a burlap sack rather than just a creel.

After catching the codfish, Mickey had wanted to stop at the pond to try his luck at catching a few more trout. It was late afternoon before they had called it a day. Mickey set off to walk the railway tracks into town, but JW had decided to take one more look at the lake before heading home.

He'd stood on the railway tracks looking at the land mass across the lake, guessing it to be a couple of miles, perhaps a little more. With the raft, they had explored a bit over there, but JW longed for the day he might sail even farther and see what was on the other side of those hills.

Out of the corner of his eye, he'd seen movement and turned to see the old man straightening the raft into a lean-to again. JW slid down the embankment and walked the short distance to where the man stood. JW saw him tense as the shore rock crunched beneath his feet, alerting the man to his presence.

"Who are you?" JW asked.

The man looked at JW and seemed to consider his words before answering.

"Just an old man out for an adventure."

JW smiled at his words. The man spoke with a slight accent. "And where will this adventure take you?"

"Here and there. I plan to keep to the tracks to see where they take me."

"I saw you earlier here at the raft," JW said.

"Yes, is it yours?"

JW nodded.

"I hope you don't mind. I was a little tired and wanted a rest out of the elements."

"I don't mind."

JW felt that the old man was done speaking, and turned to leave. "Goodbye, enjoy your adventure."

How curious, JW thought. On his walk home, he realized he hadn't gotten the man's name, nor had he given his own.

—

The old man watched as JW climbed the embankment with an ease only the youth are capable of. He would have to look for a simpler route to get back up to the train tracks. He had considered staying under the shelter of the raft, but it was likely to be a clear night; there were no clouds in the sky, and the quarter moon this evening would provide enough light to make his way. The rocks shifted under his weight as he picked his way along the sloping beach.

Nearing the railroad trestle he stepped around a burlap sack that was half in and half out of the water, absentmindedly prodding it with his staff. The sack appeared to move on its own accord, as though alive.

Thinking he had imagined it and not knowing what he might find, he bent over and cautiously began untying the baling twine that held the sack shut. It was too tight, so he pulled a small knife from his pocket, cut the knot and slowly opened the bag. Immediately a stench washed over him, and he staggered back at the sight of perhaps a half dozen tiny kittens and an equal number of fist-sized rocks. All sodden. All dead. Someone had callously put the unwanted kittens in the sack and dropped them off the trestle into the lake. He knew that people committed such acts but had never seen it for himself. Dead before their lives could begin in earnest.

Such disregard for life was nothing new, but he practiced what his mother had taught him. He respected all living things and gave thanks when he had to take a fish or animal's life and only took what he knew would get eaten.

He carried the bag over to the side of the embankment and pulled a large rock aside. He removed some dirt from the resulting hole to make a spot where he could bury the little kittens. He ignored the tear that made its way down his cheek as he thought of the little value that was put on life. He knew times were tough, but surely homes could have been found for the kittens.

He lifted the bag and gently laid it in the hole. As he started to put the earth over it, the sack moved again. He pulled the bag open and was shocked to see a little head looking up at him, mewling. He reached in and pulled the little one out. Placing the kitten on the grass, he took a second look in the sack to make sure there were no others alive. He quickly covered the bag in the hole with dirt and placed the rock back on top to keep the scavengers away.

A small freshwater brook ran to the lake, and he dipped some water into a little tin cup he carried with him. He then gathered some dry pieces of wood and started a small fire so he could warm the water. He didn't want to wash the kitten in the cold water.

He wondered how long it had been in the bag and thought it unlikely that it would survive, but that was not up to him. The water warmed, he splashed it over the little one washing away the vomit and feces that soaked its fur, trying to wash away the smell of death. Drying her with a rag from his pack, he smiled as she started purring.

"Vous êtes belle chaton. I'll call you Beauté."

After adding a little bit of sugar, he gave her a small amount of the warm water to drink, but he knew he'd have to find her something to eat. He had noticed a sparrow flitting around a tree close to where he'd buried the other kittens. He looked in the branches of the trees and saw a small nest with several eggs in it. He apologized to the mother bird, who watched him reach into the nest and flew ever closer in her desire to protect her eggs. He took only a single egg.

Holding Beauté in his palm, he cracked the egg, tipped her head back and poured the contents down her throat. She smacked her lips as the egg made its way to her stomach. Feeling badly for the mother bird but wishing for Beauté to survive, he took another egg and repeated the action. He hoped the food would make her stronger. He laid the kitten on the grass, and she wobbled over to the warm water and drank some more. She wobbled back to where he sat, climbed into his outstretched hand and went to sleep.

Chapter 7

JW heard the whinny from Lightning as he entered the yard that evening after studying with Beth. It was full dark now with only a quarter moon to show the way to the barn. The few stars seemed to be winking as clouds moved across the night's sky. JW felt his breath catch in his throat as he pulled the door closed behind him; for a moment, it was like he was back in the mine without a head-lamp to show his way. His quickened pulse made him feel like the boy who'd waited for Red to rescue him from the darkness on his first night underground, and he didn't like the feeling. He'd never forgotten to light his headlamp after that night. The absence of light had been totally disorient-ing, the brief moment of panic overwhelming.

"Hey, Lightning, old boy. What's the matter?" JW said in a voice he hoped sounded more confident than he felt at the moment. As his eyes adjusted to the lack of light, he could make out shadows in the barn. In the dim light he saw that the stall was clean and there was enough hay for the night. Petting Lightning, he whispered soothingly that ev-erything was alright and turned to leave the barn. From the corner of his eye, he saw a shadow move toward the door.

"Hey," JW called out, as someone pushed open the door and started off running through the field. "Hold up," he said and started running. He quickly caught up with the person. Grabbing the shoulder, he spun around what turned out to be a frightened old man.

"I'm sorry. I didn't steal anything. I was trying to get out of the cold for the night. I would have been gone before morning. I'm just passing through. I'll be on my way now, if you'll let me."

JW looked at the man. He was the same one he'd met earlier on the beach. He appeared older and looked tired; JW was sure he must be hungry as well. "There's no need to run off, sir. I'm sure my ma and da wouldn't want you to leave. Come on to the house, and I'll make you a cup of tea. I'm sure there are at least some biscuits for a lunch."

"We meet again. No, thank you. I don't want to be any bother."

"It's no bother, we share here," offered JW.

"Well, a cup of tea would be appreciated. But if you could just bring it out to me without your folks knowing about it, I'd be thankful. Name's Lejeune. Pierre Alfred Lejeune, but everyone calls me Alfred."

"I'm John Wallace Donaldson, sir, but everyone calls me JW– everyone except my mother." JW reached out, and they shook hands. "Well, Mr. Lejeune, let's go to the house. Ma and Da are in bed for the night, so nobody'll know about you until I tell them."

The old man slowed his pace, leaning more on his walking stick as he neared the door, approaching cautiously as Gulliver rose up from his place by the entrance. He seemed to relax as Gulliver's tailed wagged, and he reached his hand out for Gulliver to sniff.

JW made his way to the kitchen. The lamp was still on, the wick turned really low. JW knew his parents had been expecting him soon. He was glad the stew pot was still at the back of the stove, and that it was half full. He dipped up a bowl for each of them and took some biscuits out of the cupboard. JW placed the food before the old man, who followed JW's movements with his eyes, eagerly awaiting his cue to begin eating.

JW watched as the old man bowed his head in thanks, mouthing a few silent words. He ate slowly, savouring each mouthful, stopping only briefly to extend a compliment.

"This is just like my Jenean used to make. Thank you."

JW saw tears well up in the old man's eyes. He thought perhaps they were at the memory of his Jenean – or maybe because someone would extend a little kindness to an old man. He noticed Alfred was reluctant to eat the last bit on his plate.

"Eat up," JW said. "There's lots more in the pot."

"Oh, I couldn't eat another bite. I am just sorry to see the night coming to conclusion. I must get on my way."

"Well, have some more tea, and please tell me a little about yourself."

"My story, I don't think is very interesting, but I will tell some of it, if you'd like, and more tea would be nice, thank you." JW poured some tea, and the old man quietly began to speak. "I grew up on the other side of the Island and spent much of my time working the land and on the sea. I'm good with my hands, but now I'm old and ... alone. My wife, Jenean, passed a couple of years ago, and we were never blessed with children. We lived on her people's land, and her brother's son and his wife recently returned to the Island and needed the house. Oh, they offered me a room, but I guess I was a little too proud or ... angry, so I set out for Boston. I have a brother there. I thought I would hop on a freight train, but I've since learned I am too old to run after trains, and I cannot hop like I used to."

JW burst out laughing but stopped quickly, not wanting to wake his parents or offend Mr. Lejeune. He had laughed thinking of how quickly he'd caught up to the old man. When Alfred saw the now serious look on JW's face, he started to laugh, and soon both of them were chuckling.

"I planned to stay close to the train tracks," Alfred continued. "I found your raft last evening for shelter. When I saw your barn off in the field, I hoped I could just slip in and out of it undiscovered. I've taken up enough of your time. It's late, and I should be on my way. I'm sure I can find shelter along the way, and with a full stomach, I should be able to walk for hours."

JW watched as the old man tried to force his eyes wide open, as if to show that he was ready to set out on a journey. He looked closely at the old man and the silken grey whiskers that neatly covered his chin. For a moment, he thought of Tennyson's grey whiskers and wondered if perhaps both were close to the end of their life. He pushed the thought away.

"Let's go back to the barn. It's warm, and you can spend the night before heading out again," JW said, and Alfred gave a grateful nod.

JW walked ahead of Alfred and opened the door to the barn. He let the old man enter before him. "Sit there," JW said, pointing toward a bench. "I'll be right back."

A shed and small forge stood in the field adjacent to the barn, about twenty feet away, hidden from view of the house. The forge was his grandfather's. He had been dead more than ten years now, which was about how long it had been since the forge had been in use. It was strategically placed to ensure that no sparks could reach the barn, where the dry hay would ignite. The shed had been called into action now and then when his father was restless after a tiresome back shift shovelling coal and needed the solitude to sleep. Now, as overman, JW's father seldom used the cot.

"I cleared away some stuff, and got a little fire going in what used to be my grandfather's work shed," JW told Alfred. "There's a single cot in there with clean bedclothes on it. You're welcome to rest up there for the night. I don't see your belongings?"

"I dropped my pack in the field by the barn," Alfred said, and looked at JW.

"I'll go look for it. Be right back," JW said, and left to get it. It had gotten darker since they'd gone in the house. JW wasn't sure where to look but figured Alfred had only run about fifteen feet before JW had reached him, so he thought his pack should be easy to find. Squinting, JW saw a small sack a few feet from the barn. Picking it up by the twine, he swung it around his back. He felt something move and then heard a small squeal. He lowered the sack to the ground and saw a little head pop out. A young kitten looked at him in the darkness. JW thought it looked too young to even be weaned from its mother, and he wondered what Alfred was doing with a baby kitten. He put the kitten in one hand and carried the pack in the other.

Opening the shed door, JW was surprised to see how clean Alfred had made it look in a matter of minutes. It had been swept, and the teapot he'd filled was on the stove.

"Oh, I see you've found my friend," Alfred said.

JW had put some biscuits and a jar of milk on the counter so Alfred could have breakfast before he left in the morning. JW put a little of the milk in a small tin bowl and laid it on the floor for the kitten. He couldn't help smiling at the black face smeared with the cow's milk. He doubted Gulliver or Tennyson would be too pleased with the kitten, but since it was only for the night, he didn't think it would matter too much.

"Perhaps you'd like to keep her," said Alfred. "I see you have a cow, so she'd have lots to eat. Once she gets bigger she would be able to keep the mice and rat population down. I found her ... on my travels. You're welcome to her if you want. She has been good company, but I don't have much to feed her."

"No, I don't think she'd feel too welcome here with Gulliver or— Well, I think it best she go with you."

Chapter 8

The twenty minute walk to church was refreshing. The bell began its loud clanging, calling the parishioners from their rest, letting them know the service was about to begin. JW sat with his parents, and Beth sat across the aisle with her mother and sister. JW was anxious to tell Beth about Alfred, and the cat. He didn't know if the cat had a name but knew Tennyson wouldn't be too pleased to see it. Afterwards, hurrying down the steps of the church, JW knew he'd have a few minutes before his parents would start on the walk home.

"After I left you last night and got to my yard, I heard Lightning fussing in the barn. I went in and everything seemed alright, but then I saw something move, and the next thing, someone rushed out of the barn. I caught up to him, and it was an old man," JW said.

"Really?" said Beth.

"Yes. I forgot to tell you last evening, I met him on the beach earlier in the day, after Mickey had left. He said he was out for an adventure and was following the railroad tracks. Once you mentioned what Davey had said, I forgot everything.... But I learned last night that Alfred, Mr. Lejeune, is from the other side of the Island. I fed him, and he's staying in Grandpa's work shed. It has a bed and stove in it. I straightened it up a little for him, but he swept it clean. Ma and Da don't know about him yet. I even put some milk down for his kitten."

"Kitten? He's got a kitten? I'd like to see that. Do you think he'd mind if I came over later to see it?"

"I don't imagine Alfred— Mr. Lejeune would mind. He said he's on his way to Boston, so I don't know how long he'll be around. But he does look pretty tired. He sure has a good appetite. I dipped him up as much as me, and he only left a single forkful," JW said. "He offered me his kitten, but I told him that Gulliver wouldn't be too happy about a cat around. I didn't mention Tennyson, but can you picture a cat and a rat? Gullie and Tennyson barely tolerate each other."

"I could make room for the kitten, if Mr. Lejeune wants to part with it. The barn is clean and dry. I mean, if he doesn't want to keep it," Beth said.

"I'm not sure. He did say she was company for him. I think maybe he thought giving her to me would be a sort of repayment for the food and place to stay. But we could ask."

"Oh no, we better not, or he might feel like he has to give her up. But I could still go over and see her later."

"Maybe you could come over now for lunch."

Beth swept her arm the length of her body. "Not exactly the attire to play with a kitten," she said. "I'll go home first and hurry over after a quick lunch. Wait! Why didn't you tell your parents? He's not a criminal, is he?"

"No, he just seems like a tired old man who doesn't want a fuss made over him, is all, I think," JW said.

The afternoon went by quickly. Beth was enthralled with the kitten.

"I call her Beauté, ah, Beauty, because she is so tiny and dainty." Alfred decided against telling Beth the gruesome details of how she came to be with him. "I found her and cleaned her up. She is so young, I was afraid to leave her alone, for fear an animal would hurt or kill her. When I picked her up, she started to purr, so that is why I have her."

"Oh, she is a beauty," Beth said, watching the way the kitten stayed next to Alfred's feet.

"Perhaps it would be best if she stayed with you where she could have food and milk as she needs it," Alfred said.

Smiling, Beth said, "She looks like she knows where she wants to be."

Alfred smiled down at the kitten.

"I should really be going. It's almost suppertime," Beth said reluctantly.

"I'll walk you home," said JW, but he also lingered a little longer.

The old man began to pack up his few belongings. He moved his clothes aside and made a pouch for Beauty to fit in. JW felt a cool breeze come in through the open door.

"Why not stay another night? Get some more rest and start out fresh in the morning."

"I should go. I do not wish to overstay my welcome."

"Please stay if you'd like. If you do, I'll bring you some food after I walk Beth home, and I'll get in some wood for the night. There's enough to keep the fire going for now."

JW thought he saw the look of relief on the old man's face; he seemed ready to settle in for the night.

As JW and Beth slowly walked the distance to Beth's house, Gulliver bounded alongside, occasionally crashing into the woods in pursuit of a rabbit or squirrel then quickly returning to his master's side. The woods between Beth's and JW's houses were well-known to Gullie, and if a deer or lynx came through, he made it his business to keep a watchful eye. He was used to the deer running from him, and he liked to chase after them, knowing full well he could never catch them.

Once, when the much smaller lynx had run from him, he'd decided to chase it as well, and was perplexed when it stopped, turned and swiped at his nose, which left a deep gash. It even followed him as he made his way back to the house. Once Gulliver was in the clearing, the lynx had stopped the chase. Gulliver gave it a long look, knowing he would be ready the next time. He tapped his nose, the scar prominent, against JW's hand and then Beth's, searching for attention.

Twilight came, and before long stars began to speckle the sky as the three sauntered along together.

Chapter 9

"So how many fish did you and JW catch?" Patty asked, as he and Mickey walked toward the rake.

"About a dozen trout, and they were good eatin'. Then we went over to the Rock and caught seven or eight cod. Two of them were almost three feet long. We're thinking 'bout going back next week or the week after. You're welcome to come if you're not working. We plan on salting some," Mickey said.

The boys turned at the sound of raised voices and saw a boy, younger and smaller than Patty. Amid the muffled comments, they heard, "New blood!" "Special seat up front!"

"Poor fellow," Mickey said.

"Yeah," Patty said, but Mickey thought he saw relief on his friend's face. Finally, there was someone smaller than him for the men to pick on.

JW's father said, "Mick, Patty, keep an eye on young Donnie here. Start him on your door, Mick, and then work him back to Patty's door. I want him down for a few nights before he goes on his own."

"Sure, Andy," Mickey said. For almost three years now, he had been calling JW's father by his first name, as was the custom underground. "Sir" or "Mr." was not something even the younger miners had to use. They were free to use first, last or nicknames like the older miners did. Mickey now found it hard to call JW's father "Mr. Donaldson," even when they were on the surface.

Donnie stood off to one side, a look of fear on his face as he listened to the men talking about the darkness and about boys getting lost in the mine and wandering around, never to be found.

Patty draped an arm over Donnie's shoulder. "Don't pay any attention to those guys. Some of them wet their pants the first night they went down below. Most of them squealed like babies the first time on the rake," Patty said, remembering his own fateful first night. "You ever been on the rake before?" he asked, pointing to the small tram cars that looked like little railway cars.

Donnie shook his head.

"Well this here's the rake, or trip, and it's how we get back and forth from the workings." Patty whispered, "Don't let on I told you, but they sit all the first-timers at the front of the trip, and then they let the thing travel lickety-split, fast as it can go, to scare the devil out of them. Try not to make a sound, but don't worry if you do. I made a small noise the first time. Just keep your head down and your eyes closed."

Andy and Mickey smiled when Patty said he'd made only a small noise on his first trip, remembering he'd squealed like the frightened child he'd been. Andrew was glad Patty had befriended Donnie. His smallness would make him a target for some of the not-so-friendly miners, though he was sure that the likes of Smitty and other adult miners would extend some kindness.

Andy had heard that Smitty's parents had moved to Whitney Pier and were thinking of opening up a private school, like they'd run in Barbados. He hoped Smitty would not follow anytime soon but expected he might. The steel plant in the Pier would provide an opportunity for Smitty to have a job above ground, and Andrew knew there were others from Barbados working there, perhaps some of Smitty's friends from his home country. His skills and good nature would be a terrible loss if he did decide to go.

The rake started loading, and Andrew watched the small fellow square his shoulders and take a deep breath before taking the solitary seat at the front. Donnie glanced back and caught Patty's eye and gave a small smile, then lowered his head as the descent began. He never made a sound.

Chapter 10

JW walked quickly from school, confident that he and Beth had both done well on the math test.

"Slow down, JW," Beth said. "What's your hurry?"

"Sorry," JW said, taking Beth by the hand. "I'm just hoping that Alfred hasn't left yet. I was going to pack him a lunch to take with him. He stayed all weekend, but I expect him gone any time."

Beth smiled at him. "Well, let's hurry then."

They broke into a run, and when they arrived at Beth's, she went in her house and returned with bread and cake. She'd cut the bread in slices.

"This should help with the lunch," Beth said.

"Thanks, it sure will." He kissed her, then turned to leave. Then he turned back and kissed her a second time. "Thanks again. See you in the morning."

Beth watched JW run up the hill and smiled when he stopped at the top to see if she was still outside. She waved, as did he, and then he began running again. She heard his shrill whistle and was sure Gullie would soon be barrelling toward JW. *He's such a special boy, I mean, young man*, she thought, and walked inside to help her mother with supper.

—

Mary watched from the bedroom door as Andrew tossed in his sleep. She noticed sweat glistening on his forehead, and when she walked closer, she saw that his hair and even the pillow were wet. She placed her hand on his forehead, and it was cold to the touch. He shivered, and she drew the blanket to his chin and laid her hand on his chest, which seemed to relax him. His breathing became more regular. She backed away from the bed and returned to the kitchen to finish supper for JW. *I hope he's not coming down with something*, Mary thought. She knew he would not miss time from work. His days and nights in the mine consisted of walking the tunnels, ensuring that the operations were running smoothly, if that was possible in the chaos of an underground mine. He seemed tired of late. The switch from day shift to night shift seemed more difficult for him than it used to.

Mary heard Gulliver bark as he raced down the road, signalling that JW was on the way. Her son's appetite was enormous. Mary was glad he ate so well, but it was hard to keep him full. The fishing and hunting he did helped with the food, and the garden produced enough to last them through the winter, with a surplus to be shared. Rabbit stew was still his favourite, and she dipped up a large bowl, filled to the brim, and watched the steam rise. Mary saw JW pass the kitchen window and head toward the barn. She opened the kitchen door and called to him.

"Come have a bite to eat before you clean the stalls, John Wallace," Mary said.

Looking over his shoulder, JW answered, "Be right there, Ma."

Out of sight of the house, JW hurried into his grandfather's shed and saw Alfred asleep on the cot with Beauty lying at his feet, curled in a ball. He put the food items on the work bench and backed out of the room, gently closing the door.

"That smells great, Ma," JW said as he sat at the table. He wanted to get back out to the shed and ate even more quickly than usual.

"Slow down before you choke yourself."

"It's just so good," JW said, sopping up the gravy with a piece of bread. "Well, I better get the barn cleaned. I'll bring in some wood later. I think there's enough coal in already." The temperature dropped at night, sometimes leaving frost on the windows to greet them in the early mornings.

Mary listened as JW closed the door behind him. As she pushed the stew to the back of the stove, she thought how unusual it was for him to have had only the one bowl. She smiled, thinking the rest of it could be gone once he finished his chores. As she cleared the table and washed the dishes, her mind returned to Andrew. She sighed at the thought of him sick and still trying to work.

JW saw the shed door was open. Alfred was kneeling on the floor looking under the cot. He raised himself up as JW walked into the room.

"I'm looking for the kitten. She was at my feet when I laid down, but I can't find her now."

JW felt terrible – maybe he hadn't closed the door fully when he stopped in earlier. "I'll check the barn," he said, and hurried across the open space.

He heard the old man say, "I thought I pulled the door closed so she couldn't get out."

JW watched Beauty walk across the straw-covered floor and reached to pick her up before she entered Lightning's stall. A few more feet and she would have been in grave danger. Lightning's hooves could crush her fragile skull. "We better get you back to Alfred, girl."

JW saw the relief on the old man's face as he held Beauty out to him.

"It appears she likes to wander, eh? We really should be on our way," Alfred said.

"You can stay a while longer, if you wish, but I'd have to tell my folks. It doesn't seem right keeping secrets from them. I'm sure they wouldn't mind you staying."

"I don't want to be a burden to them, and they already— I think I should get on my way to Boston."

"Is your brother expecting you?"

"I haven't seen or heard from Louis in ten years. I'm not even sure he's still there, but," Alfred reached into his small pack, pulled an envelope from it and handed it to JW, "the address shows he was in Boston then, so it is where I have to go to look for him. But, no, he is not expecting me. And, in truth, another night or two of rest would be good."

When his father sat to eat his supper, JW was at the table with a cup of tea, wondering if he should mention Alfred now or wait until his father returned in the morning. "Better eat some of that stew, Da. The nights are long down there," JW said, and smiled.

"That so."

JW nodded. "Da, Ma, a few nights ago when I was checking on Lightning, someone ran from the barn and I chased after him. It was an old man from the other side of the Island. He said he was on his way to Boston, but he looked tired and hungry, so I offered him some food. He said he didn't want to be a burden, and he didn't want me to tell you. So I fed him and let him stay in Grandpa's shed for the night. Well, he's still there. I told him he could stay longer, but that I had to tell you, because I—"

"Yes, we know about Alfred," Andrew said. "Scared the life out of your poor mother meeting him like that. She wasn't expecting someone to be living in Da's shed!"

"Yes, and I was hardly dressed for company," his mother said.

JW looked at his parents. There was no smiling or laughing, and he sensed disappointment.

"How could you expect to keep such a secret with smoke coming out of the shed's chimney early morning and again late at night?" Andrew said. "Plus your mother figured something was up when you chose to do your chores before eating. We met Alfred and decided to wait to see how long it would be before you told us."

"And you took your time," Mary said.

"I'm sorry, but he—"

"Alfred told us. We know you were just being kind, but if he was someone dangerous … well, we could be having a different conversation."

"I know, Da. He just seemed scared and tired. I was afraid he'd leave without eating if I told you right away. He said his wife died a couple of years ago, and he doesn't have any children." JW saw his mother's eyes meet his father's. "I'm sorry. It won't happen again."

Chapter 11

Donnie listened to his mother in the kitchen. He'd been awake for the past hour thinking about his upcoming shift. Tonight, he would have to work the trap door all by himself. Andy had given him two nights' training, one with Mickey and one with Patty, but tonight he was on his own. His father had left to find work after the company store had closed, when it had looked like the mines were done. That was three years ago, and they hadn't heard from him since.

Donnie had spent some time above ground at the breakers, but now he was big enough to go underground – though not old enough. But they needed the money, and his mother had signed a paper stating he was sixteen, so no more breakers. The breakers, where he'd sorted the rocks and shale from the coal, were dangerous, with coal speeding down the chutes and conveyor belts. But Donnie liked being above ground, and he'd learned to keep his hands safe, after injuring them a few times.

He was glad Patty had told him what to expect. He was still afraid but hoped he'd get used to it. Donnie pulled on his pants and shirt and went outside. Theirs was the middle one in the row of company houses – five other houses on either side of them. Except for enough to put a little food on the table for him, his little sister and mother, what he earned went to pay rent to keep a roof over their heads.

Looks like rain, he thought, and then headed back inside to wash down a couple of biscuits with some hot tea before going to the mine.

—

Beth heard the patter of rain against her window and saw a flash of lightning in the distance. She pulled the quilt to her chin and felt the warmth envelope her. In a couple of weeks, the winter quilts would be put away for some lighter bed-clothes. She wondered if Alfred and Beauty were on their way and if they had been caught in the deluge. She would have loved to have taken Beauty home with her, but she felt that the kitten was all the old man had in his life. She didn't really know anything about Alfred, other than what JW had already told her – that he had worked the land and on the sea. She thought he was a nice old man with many tales to tell, but she believed it would take time for him to share them. She hoped that he and Beauty had found shelter. She prayed they were in a dry boxcar destined for Boston.

The rain increased in its intensity, and the steady rhythm relaxed her. She thought of the kindness JW had shown Alfred, and she smiled. One more year, and they would be finished high school. For many, if not most, grade eleven – junior matriculation – was as far as they went, all most would ever need. She wanted to be a nurse. She would apply after finishing school this year and would take whatever training was necessary. JW wanted to travel the world. She wondered what that actually meant and how he'd be able to do that. His father, as overman in the mine, had a better job than before, but could they afford to send JW to college? She wondered what would become of them, her and JW. She looked forward to their summer: picnics and swimming. They were both sixteen now, and Beth knew of girls in town who'd been married by her age. The rain seemed to be letting up. She turned her face to the wall and felt sleep overtake her.

—

JW listened to the start of the rain and was glad that his father had left early, or he would have been drenched. He was relieved his parents knew about Alfred but wished he'd told them himself. He didn't usually keep secrets of any kind.

Alfred had joined them for supper, had eaten some stew and thanked them again for allowing him to stay, telling them what a wonderful son they had. He'd declined the offer of staying in a room in the house, saying the shed more than met his needs, and he was willing to work to repay their kindness. They told him he didn't have to work and that he was welcome to stay as long as he wanted.

After supper, JW had walked back to the shed with Alfred. He was glad Alfred had decided to stay for another little while. The old man seemed contrite and apologized for asking him to keep such a secret and also for keeping the secret asked by JW's parents.

"I'm sorry I got you into this. I asked you to keep a secret, which you did; your father asked me to keep a secret, which I did. I'm sorry," Alfred said again.

"I'm just glad it's out in the open now. No more secrets for me," JW said.

"Me too," Alfred said.

Now, in his bed, listening to the rain, JW thought of Beth. He remembered how she'd looked at him when she told him what Davey Brown had said. Tomorrow, he would have a heart-to-heart talk with Davey. He liked Davey okay, but he would have to let him know what's what. JW remembered his plan to make it up to Beth for his fishing trip with Mickey. In the morning, he'd ask Beth to go to the Strand Theatre on Saturday.

The rain pelted the window and the wind seemed to have picked up. He thought about the upcoming tests and the final exams that would soon follow. The summer off with Beth was what he was looking forward to. He fell asleep thinking about her.

—

"I love that JW wants to help Alfred and that he sees sharing with others as the right thing to do," Mary said.

"Yes, I know, and it's how we raised him, but sharing our surplus is easier than adding another mouth to feed. I know the meat supply is low, but I haven't felt up to hunting much lately. There's half a dozen hens that are done laying. We could roast them up or make a stew outta them, and we still have a bit of corned beef and a pretty good supply of salt fish, so we should be okay for a while," Andrew said.

"Alfred mentioned that he plans to head out for Boston soon, but I fear with that limp he may not get far," Mary said.

"Can't turn an old man away, but we may have to stretch the food a little farther. He seems to have almost as good an appetite as JW."

Despite their concern, they both chuckled at this.

Chapter 12

Patty took the seat next to Donnie. He knew the boy was scared, thinking about a night alone underground. Patty remembered his first night alone; it hadn't been fun. The darkness and the rats were bad enough, but some of the old-timers were worse.

"Don't worry, Donnie," Patty said in a low voice. "The first night's the worst. Don't pay no attention to the old fellas. Some of them are mean and cranky. Just pull the door open like me and Mick showed you, and you'll be fine."

Donnie nodded with rapt attention to every word Patty said, as always, making sure he wasn't missing any important information. "I'll do it just like you showed me. Hope the door don't get stuck."

"It shouldn't. Just be sure to lather up the hinges with the grease," Patty said, knowing the door was going to be heavy for someone the size of Donnie. "The rats won't bother you if you throw them a few crumbs."

"I will. Thanks. I don't mind the rats too much. There's lots behind our house. Sometimes you can hear them in the walls."

The rake started moving, and Patty lowered his head and watched to make sure Donnie did too. They were in the middle of the cars. No new blood tonight. The speed of the rake seemed leisurely compared to the nights when first-timers went down below. As the rake pulled to a stop, Patty waited until Donnie got his lamp lit before heading toward his door. He pulled his door open and pointed along the tracks.

"Just stay to the left and you'll reach Mick's door," Patty said.

A sudden voice behind them caused them to jump. "That's okay, Patty. I'll see young Donnie gets to his door," Andrew said.

"Evening, Andy. That's good then. See you in the mornin', Donnie," Patty said.

Andrew clapped Patty on the back and went through the door with Donnie following close behind. "Goodnight, Patty. Stay awake."

"Always do, Andy," he said. In a lower voice he added, "mostly." He let the door close and heard the scrape of metal on metal as the first tram loaded with coal made its way toward him. He remembered the lessons JW had taught him. He'd learned the importance of closing the trap door quickly to keep the fresh air down where the men were working. Fresh air was pumped into the mine from the surface. If the fresh air was gone, the men could suffocate. The thought of that scared him and kept him awake and aware most nights. Day shifts were busier, so it was easier to stay awake.

"Open the door. Not asleep already, are you?"

Patty looked into the face of Mickey's father. "No, Shawn, I'm not asleep," Patty said. He pulled the door open and let it close as soon as the tram cleared the door.

"Watch it, boy. Ya almost hit the tram," Shawn said.

Patty knew Donnie would hear the same line, unless Andy was still there. With Mickey talking about getting off the trap door, Patty was hoping he could leave too, but with little Donnie on the trap now, he thought he might have to stay a while to make sure he got along okay. He kinda liked the way Donnie looked up to him. *Yes, I think I'll wait some, before I make the move.*

—

"So that's what I'm thinking, JW. Me and you haul the coal and split her down the middle," Mickey said.

"I like the sound of that, as long as you're sure your father won't put up a fuss," JW said. "What'll he think of it?"

"The old fella's all tuckered out after a shift in the pit, and I can't do it all myself. The best I get outta him is he'll drive the wagon, but he just sits there and watches me shovel the coal on and off."

"I'll do the same for you. You do all the work and I'll collect half the money," JW said, laughing.

"I was thinking the other way around sounds better."

JW was excited at the prospect of working during the summer and making some money. "When do we start? I still have exams to write, but I can work Saturdays."

"I'm off the next two days, so I'll try to set up some deliveries," Mickey said. "I'll talk to you this evening. With all the coal shovelling you'll be doing, you'll be ready to work underground for one of the miners."

"No way. What do you mean, 'for one of the miners?'"

"Some of the miners pay young fellas out of their pay to work as drivers. Da wanted me to work for him in the pit, but there was no way I would do that."

"I thought everyone was paid by the company. No offence, but I sure wouldn't want to work for your father."

"Not many would, and those that start with him never seem to last long."

—

"Hi, Ma," JW said as he entered the kitchen. He saw she was deep in thought and had her prayer book open in front of her. He was anxious to tell her about his job working with Mickey on Saturdays until school was out, and then more days during the summer, whatever days Mickey had off and wanted to work.

"Oh hi, dear," she said, and offered a hint of a smile. She rose from the table and put her prayer book back in the cupboard.

"Is something wrong, Ma?"

"No, dear." She looked up into the face of her son and saw the worry in his eyes. He was practically grown. "It's just that your father seems tired, more than usual."

"Do you think he's okay?"

"Yes ... well ... I'm not sure. He's got the cold sweats, and I heard him coughing pretty hard today, but he said he's okay and that he just breathed in some dust last night."

"That dust can knock the good out of a fella for a couple of days, getting it out of your lungs," JW said, hopeful that's all it was. He didn't like to see his mother worrying, and he was afraid that it might be more than some dust in his father's lungs. He pushed plans with Mickey to the back of his mind. He picked up a turnip and started peeling it. He'd told his mother he wanted to know how to cook, so he'd be able to make his own meals when he was sailing on the ocean.

"The shed looks like a little house. You've fixed it up nicely," JW said.

"Oh, I am quite comfortable, and happy that your parents allow me to stay," Alfred said.

"Is there anything you need?"

"No, I have everything I need. All that is missing is my library. I miss the books I collected over the years," Alfred said.

"You like to read? So do I."

"Oh, I love to read, JW," Alfred said. "The winters can be long and harsh. Once the food was harvested for the winter and the wood cut and stacked, there were some long nights. Me and Jenean would sit by the fire reading from the books in our small library. As the firelight danced across the pages, the words would come alive and take me. Oh, listen to an old man prattle on. Forgive me."

JW looked at him in amazement. "That's how I feel about books. I love how they take me to other places, to see how others lived. I have books in my room that I can loan you. Tell me what you like to read, and I will see what's available at the library in town."

"That would be wonderful. I will prepare a list. Thank you."

Chapter 13

"Whaddaya mean I can't use the horse to haul the coal?" Mickey asked his father. "JW's gonna help me. You said you didn't want to haul it anymore."

"I'm not going to put more money in the pockets of the Donaldsons. If you was hauling it yourself, you could use the horse."

"I can't get enough done if I have to do all the work myself. JW could use the money, same as me," Mickey said.

"I'm not going to kill off our horse to put money in his pockets."

"He helped dig you out from the cave-in, Da. You seemed to like him well enough then."

The slap came quick and hard. Mickey stared at his father, silent for a moment. "I ain't a boy, and I don't expect to be treated like one," he said. "I've been doin' a man's work for a lot of years, so I expect to be treated like a man."

Shawn McGuire looked at his son, who equalled him in size and maybe even strength. His anger wasn't at JW or at his son. He just didn't like that Andy Donaldson was both his boss and his better. "You can't use it, is all."

Mickey watched his father walk to the house. He'd heard that Andy'd had to tell his father not to be hollering at the new trapper boy, Donnie. Mickey couldn't wait until he had enough money saved to get a place of his own. He'd miss his mother, brother and sisters, but he'd see more than enough of his father underground to suit him. If it was up to him, he'd haul coal on the surface rather than stand at a door all day or all night long. Mickey wanted more out of life than what his father had. He was tired of being bullied. Besides, he and Beth's cousin, Sally Young, were getting pretty serious. She planned to go into nursing with Beth, and he hoped they'd marry one day. Mickey smiled, then thought he'd better not get ahead of himself.

—

The stew would take some time to cook, so JW decided to walk into town, maybe stop by the Co-op or library. Although he hadn't told his mother, JW figured Mickey would let her know if they'd be hauling coal tomorrow.

As he neared the old graveyard, JW slowed down. He remembered the first night he'd set out for the mine alone three years ago. His father had followed behind him, bringing the lunch JW had dropped from his satchel, catching up to JW just as he came abreast of the graveyard. JW had jumped and squealed in fear, and both he and his father had had a good laugh at the thought of ghosts coming from the graveyard to get JW. He thought of the time spent at the kitchen table learning from his father about the underground workings of the mine. JW, initially thinking that it was simply grown-up stories, slowly came to the realization that his father was preparing him, wanting him to understand how the coal mine worked.

The mine owners' cutback of wages and working hours had forced JW's parents to send him to work in the mines. Many of the other families in the surrounding areas had had to do the same. JW had been fortunate to be able to get out of the mine and return to school after only a few months. Others weren't so fortunate. JW appreciated that both his mother and father had done everything they could to get him back to school. One more year and he would be off to college, and then ... off to see the world.

JW saw the door to the library was open. Mrs. Johnson was still doing double duty, teaching during the days and ensuring the adults and older children had a place to get some reading materials in the evenings. Mrs. Johnson had taught him until grade eight and was still his favourite teacher.

The roughly hewn table had several books on it. JW saw a book that interested him. He'd read it before but decided to read it again. He flipped the book open to the front page and became engrossed in the familiar tale. He heard someone clearing his throat and looked up into the eyes of JB McLachlan.

"It's good to see you reading, son," JB said.

JW saw JB straining to read the title. "It's Ivanhoe, sir. I like to read about the history of heroes."

"Heroes aren't the knights and kings of old," McLachlan seemed to scoff. "The men who work to earn the money and the women who raise the children and see they are fed – they are heroes. Those are the things that should be taught in schools. Look at William Davis. There's a hero," JB said.

JW was familiar with the story. He'd been told William Davis had been shot and killed while out getting a bottle of milk for his baby. He didn't understand how that made him a hero.

JB saw the perplexed look on JW's face. "There are differing stories of what happened: that he was looking for his son, was on the picket line, or the most popular one, that he was getting milk for his baby. But, don't you see, it doesn't matter. Davis represents the working man, doing what's needed to take care of his family."

JW nodded, thinking of the nights his own father got out of his warm bed to head into the black coal mine, just so they could eat. "Yes, sir. I do see what you mean."

JB continued. "The conditions here are still terrible, but it wasn't too many years ago that kids five and six years old were in the coal mines – boys and girls, and lots were hauling coal."

JW saw the veins standing out on JB's neck as he became more passionate. He believed that JB truly cared for every man and boy – or girl – that went underground.

"Girls too?" JW asked, incredulous, thinking he meant the local mines.

"Yes, girls too, and they weren't treated very well. That was back in Scotland and Ireland and other places as well,

I'm sure. I don't know if that happened here, but it wouldn't surprise me."

"Sounds terrible," JW said. He didn't bother mentioning that Long Jack had told him about the young girls working in the mines in Scotland, England and Wales. He didn't feel the need to say much, once JB got started on a topic.

"Aye, it was terrible, lad, but that's why we have to keep working for the rights. Those mine owners would put babies in the mines, if they thought they could make a penny off their blood, sweat and tears."

JW knew the times were hard and that the wages still left a lot to be desired. His own father was working regular hours, so JW hadn't paid much attention to what was going on with the other workers. His parents still shared any surplus vegetables, milk and cheese, but he never considered how bad things might be in other people's lives.

"I'm not saying or implying for you to stop reading books about knights and kings, but spend some time learning the history of the working men – and women. That's where you'll learn about real heroes."

"I have the book you requested, Mr. McLachlan," Mrs. Johnson said from her desk.

JB walked over and picked up the book. He thanked her and took the book, grunting in satisfaction. "We'll talk again soon, JW. Say hello to your father."

"Yes, sir. G'bye, sir," JW said. He watched McLachlan walk up the street. His fiery temper was the same, but JW's father had told him that the time JB had spent in prison, for sticking up for the miner's rights, had hurt him physically – that he'd gotten ill with tuberculosis and never fully recovered or regained the vigour he'd once possessed.

Whenever JW spent time speaking with JB, he felt a stirring of indignation, anger at how the men had been treated. Having learned that even young children, including girls, had worked underground, JW was beginning to believe that the mine owners truly didn't care if the men and their families lived or died. He remembered Red telling him that the horses and ponies used to haul the coal cars are treated better than the men, because the animals cost money and the men are free. "And abundant," JW said to himself in a low voice.

He laid Ivanhoe on the table. Perhaps he would get it out during the summer months. Right now, he had lots of school books to read. Alfred had declined getting books from the library until he'd finished reading the books JW had loaned him. Thinking about what Mr. McLachlan said, JW remembered the library book he still had at home, *The Bitter Cry of the Children*. Maybe he would finally get to read it over the summer. Hauling coal with Mickey, spending time with Beth swimming and having picnics, and planting and tending the garden wouldn't leave a lot of time to get much reading done, but he'd squeeze in some.

"Good bye, Mrs. Johnson," JW said, heading for the door.

"Bye, JW," she said, and waved as he left the library.

—

The old man's hand pulled the knife blade slowly along the piece of wood. Small cuts at various angles carved an intricate design. Taking the tool kit from his pack, Alfred found the chisel he wanted. He tapped it lightly against the wood and watched his carving begin to take shape. He had seen some carvings of wooden ships at various stages, some almost complete, in the shed where he was staying. Although they weren't quite to scale, he thought the sculptor had potential and with a little instruction and practice would be very good.

The fine detailed work of his younger years required a strength he no longer possessed, and Alfred felt his fingers cramp after a short period of time working on the piece. The schooner he was carving was a bit too ambitious to complete in a few days. He had told JW and Mr. and Mrs. Donaldson that he would be leaving for Boston shortly. He looked around the little shed, watched Beauty chase a spider into a corner then pounce on it as it attempted to climb the wall. He smiled. The kitten seemed perplexed with her capture, unsure what to do now that she had it in her paws. He listened to the bubbling teapot and moved it to the back of the stove, away from the heat. Alfred looked at the piece of wood again and picked it up. *Perhaps the trip to Boston can wait a while*, he thought.

Chapter 14

"Da, can I use Lightning to haul coal with Mickey? Shawn, I mean, Mr. McGuire won't let him use their horse. Mickey says he has a few customers now, and we're hoping to get a few more for the summer."

Andrew looked across the table at his son. He seemed to be growing every day, as was his appetite. Two helpings of everything was the usual for JW, but Andrew had to force himself to bring each forkful to his mouth. Whatever was ailing him had taken a really good hold. He dreaded walking the tunnels while feeling this poorly.

"Sure, just be sure to take it easy on the old boy. He's not getting any younger," Andrew said, smiling.

"Thanks, Da. We will. At least he can have some more oats, 'cause he'll get lots of exercise."

"What are you planning to do with all your money?"

"I'm going to start saving for college, but I might have to spend a little taking Beth to the Strand for a matinee or two. Can't leave a pretty girl like Beth alone too long, or some other boy might try to steal her," JW said, thinking of Davey Brown. He was going to use Davey's words to Beth as a lesson for himself and be sure to pay closer attention to her.

JW pulled his satchel from his bookcase. The last few weeks had sped by so quickly. He hoped the summer would go more slowly. He'd told Beth about the work he'd be doing with Mickey but that he would have lots of time for swimming and picnics with her once he tended the garden. To himself, he wondered where he'd find the extra hours in his days.

JW was glad Alfred was still in the work shed. The old man had attempted to leave a few times, but his pride stood in his way because he wouldn't accept money to buy a ticket. Instead, he tried to leave by walking the tracks, with the hope of climbing into a slow-moving boxcar. Once he'd even managed to board a boxcar, only to have it shunted to a line ten miles from where he'd started. After spending the night in the car, he realized it wouldn't be moving anytime soon. It had taken him a day and a half of walking to get back to the barn.

When JW's father mentioned that they might have to hire someone to help with the harvest this year, Alfred quickly offered his services. His new plan was to help with the garden to earn his keep and work through the harvest, hopefully earning enough to buy a ticket. JW had learned a few gardening tricks from him and liked how the beans followed the trellises that Alfred had constructed.

From the crest of the hill, JW saw that Beth was waiting for him. All thoughts of the garden left him. He absently patted Gullie and told him to go home, then ran down the hill. His hand slipped into Beth's, and they started on their way to school and the last day of grade eleven.

"I've made up my mind. I plan to go in to be a nurse, JW," Beth said.

"Good. That will come in handy while we travel the world," JW said. His plans had changed from his mother and father travelling with him to just Beth. She had mentioned becoming a nurse before, but now she was clearly ready to pursue it.

"Or if we decide to live around here. I'm going to put in an application."

"I want to be an engineer and build – or maybe a carpenter," JW said, remembering that to become an engineer would cost a lot of money and a carpenter a lot less. "I still want to travel, but maybe after working for a few years." JW still believed what Mrs. Johnson had told him, that with an education he could do anything, but he was coming to realize that not everyone could afford an education. "With the two of us working and saving for a few years, we could save enough to ship out to Africa or Europe."

"Perhaps. Or maybe we could travel to Ontario to see Niagara Falls. That would be nice," Beth said.

"Sure, that would be nice, but ... yes, that would be nice," JW said. He realized that Beth was only trying to be realistic. "Yeah, Niagara Falls would be a great place to start, then Victoria Falls in Africa."

Beth smiled. "Yes, then Victoria Falls."

—

School was now finished for the year and grade eleven was a thing of the past. Hauling coal with Mickey had made these last weeks fly by. It was hard work, but the money made it worth it. Both JW and Beth had done really well on their exams and were looking forward to the summer off.

JW stood looking up at the high school. Although he was happy the school year was over – happier still that he had passed – he felt a sense of loss. He enjoyed going to school each day and loved learning new things. Since he'd been old enough to read, JW had a book in his hands whenever he had the chance.

He remembered that even when Mickey had been in school, his friend had seen books, scribblers and pencils as torturers' tools, and homework as punishment. Although their elementary teacher, Mrs. Johnson, had told everyone about the importance of school and how an education could open up new worlds for them, few took her words to heart. JW realized that most children of coal miners would have been indoctrinated into that culture at an early age and would see a pick and shovel in their future, with little time to dream. He was so grateful he'd been able to go to school and that he was facing a future where he got to choose what he wanted to do. He'd certainly never choose to go underground again.

JW sat on his bed and listened to his father's hacking cough. Andrew seemed to be getting worse with each passing day. He joined them at mealtimes only for the sake of appearance, going through the motions of lifting the food to his mouth but putting most back on his plate. JW got under the covers, hoping and praying that his father would get better. When the coughing subsided, JW drifted off into a fitful sleep.

Chapter 15

"Didn't expect to ever see you down here again," Smitty said.

"It was never in my plans, Smitty, but with Da ... you know," JW said.

Smitty nodded, not knowing what to say. He chuckled, "Now you're bigger than the door. The size of you, you'll never have to worry about the door sticking on you."

"Yeah, the tunnel ceilings seem to be a lot lower these days, and I don't like the trip any better. Still seems to travel pretty fast."

Smitty smiled. "Wait until you go down tunnel twelve, it's a cage they use there. Listen, I'll try to drop by and give you a hand with some of the work around the farm until your pa gets better."

"Thanks, Smitty. I'll be alright."

The familiar sound of another tram approaching halted their conversation, and JW opened the door to begin his first shift underground in almost three years. He was glad he wouldn't have to face Shawn McGuire. Mickey said he was working dayshift this week.

JW looked up the tunnel. Although it was the same one he'd spent months in before, the familiarity didn't give him any pleasure. He looked at the wall where he had pulled the shale away years ago to create an opening large enough for his satchel. The opening was still there. He'd have to clean it a little, but it would keep the satchel dry and away from the scurrying rats.

This time there was no soft-spoken overman to make the first night bearable. Instead, there was a gruff man who pointed the way to the door and said, "Pull it open, push it closed. Nothing else to know."

JW started to tell him he'd done the job before, but the man was already walking away. He hadn't bothered to introduce himself or ask JW his name. The long shadows cast by his headlamp sent a shiver up JW's spine, especially when he saw the rats dancing in the light. He wished he hadn't read Mary Shelley's Frankenstein and Bram Stoker's Dracula.

—

Mary Donaldson dried her face, wiping away the tears she didn't want her husband to see. Barely three months ago Andrew had appeared fit as a fiddle, but then coughing fits robbed him of most of his strength and eating so little stole the rest. His clothes hung on him like on a scarecrow. Try as he might, he had to stop going to work. She had watched him argue with JW against his going back to work in the mine.

"It's not right that you go there. All your hard work studying, you hafta go back to school in the fall," Andrew had told his son.

"By then, you'll be back on your feet, Da, and I'll go back."

That had seemed to calm Andrew. Mary did see some improvement in him, and she'd been relieved when the doctor said it wasn't tuberculosis, it was pneumonia. One of his lungs had partially cleared up, but the other was barely allowing any air into it at all. The doctor said it could take a while. "It might get better," he'd said, but quickly added, "it might not."

Mary prayed that her husband's lungs would heal, but she knew he was a long way from being well enough to return to work. She was sure even old Alfred could beat him in a foot race. Now, she was glad Alfred was still with them. He tended the garden and looked after the animals, even making sure that JW's pet rat Tennyson was fed.

She hadn't seen fear or disappointment on JW's face as he'd readied himself for his first shift. But he was sixteen and bigger than most of the men in town, so she didn't expect him to show it. She just hated that reality had to make him rethink his dreams. She knew his father's illness and the fact that the cost of a college education was beyond their means must be weighing heavy on him. Mary poured a cup of tea, took her prayer book and sat at the kitchen table. She opened it to her favourite prayer and began to read.

—

"Kate, when I look at the boy, I see an intelligence and ... it's like he's an old soul. He's only fifteen or sixteen, but he sees injustice in the way others are treated. He shouldn't ever have to work in the mines; he should be working for the men. Each time I see him at the library, he's got a different book in his hands. He has a thirst for knowledge and is like a sponge soaking it all up. He seemed quite indignant when I told him that young girls in Britain worked the coal mines." JB looked at his wife, and smiled while he waited for her to speak.

"James Bryson McLachlan, you're going after them a little young for your cause, aren't you?" Kate said.

"Never too early to learn right from wrong, dear."

"At least your version of it, James," Kate said, smiling. "Why don't you have a little lie-down before supper? I'll call you when it's ready."

She watched as he shuffled from the room. He had the heart of a lion, and although they had broken him physically during his stay in jail in 1923, his spirit was as strong as ever, or stronger. She knew he loved his family above all, but she would never ask him to choose between them or the miners. Fighting for miners' rights had been his life's work, and even with his failing health, she supported him fully.

—

"Hiya, Patty," JW said, slapping him on the back.

"JW. I never thought I'd see you back here," Patty said.

"Me neither." JW looked at the faces of the men and boys waiting for the trip to take them below. He had heard the same or similar comment from most of the men who knew him. "But it's been more than a week and a half so far." He didn't really mind the rake, but he had to bend a lot lower these days. If not, the overhead beams would take off the top of his head.

"Looks like you grew another foot since I saw you last month. Don't think I'd want to wrestle with you these days," Patty said, smiling.

JW looked at the slightly built Patty and thought he hadn't changed much since they'd first met almost three years ago. They had been pretty much the same size then. At six foot two inches, JW figured he was just about done growing. Perhaps the fresh air had helped him grow, and the pit had stunted Patty's growth. Perhaps his spirit as well, although JW saw that he was still quick with a smile. "Probably not a good idea. Especially since we don't have Red to give us a break if we got caught," JW said.

"Didn't ya hear? The company asked him to come back while your Pa's off."

"No. I never heard that."

"Yeah, someone said they asked him today. Right now, Anderson is doing the job," Patty said. "He came from the other side. Never says much. All he does is grunt. How's your Pa doing?"

"He seems to be getting a little better, but it'll be a while before he can walk the tunnels. That's why I'm here."

"I hope he gets better soon," Patty said. "But it's nice having you back, if only for a little while."

"Yeah, I hope it's only for a little while." JW believed that his father was still a long way from being ready to return to work and that he would be working with no end in sight.

"Mickey's back tomorrow night. It'll be just like old times," Patty said. "He keeps talking about moving off the trap door, but it's easy, so I don't know why he would. Although I heard that he and Sally are talking about getting hitched."

"What? Who told you that?"

"My ears are closer to the ground, so I hear everything," Patty said, laughing. "Time to get aboard."

JW watched a young fellow walk their way.

"JW, this here's Donnie. He's been here a while now. Knows the ropes, but don't much like it."

"Can't say I blame him. What's to like, eh, Donnie?"

"Well, I don't mind the rats or the work. But, to be honest, the darkness and the wind bringing the voices from below every time I open the door make the hair on my neck stand up. Some of the other miners said that some trapper boys left their doors and got lost down in the deeps, and that's the voices I'm hearing," Donnie said.

JW looked at Patty. Before JW had worked his first shift, Patty had told him about trapper boys being lost in the tunnels.

"Don't look at me," Patty said. "I never told him that. I said it's just a story to try and scare the new boys." Patty saw JW's look and added, "Honest."

Still, the thought of voices coming through the tunnels made JW a little uneasy. "That's just talk, like Patty said. They want to scare the new folks, probably because they went through the same thing. Some of them might still be scared," JW said. He thought he saw Donnie relax a little. It was mean to scare people when they had no choice but to be there. "How old are you, Donnie?"

"Sixteen," Donnie said. He looked behind him then lowered his voice. "I'll be fourteen next month, but Ma said I'm to tell everyone I'm sixteen 'cause we need the money real bad since Da left. Ma keeps looking out the window and telling the younger ones that Da could be back any day now. It's been a long time since.... I don't expect him back, least ways, not soon. He's been gone three years. I worked at the breakers for almost two years. Wish I was still there."

JW didn't like to be back in the mine, but he knew he was far better off than poor Donnie. Patty took the seat beside JW, and Donnie sat behind them. "What's tunnel twelve like?" JW asked.

"The tunnel's okay, but getting there is scary," Patty said. "You gotta go down, straight down – more than eight hundred feet – in a cage held by a wire rope. The trip moves at a snail's pace compared to the cage. Feels like your stomach stays at the top when your body's at the bottom. Lots of breakfasts on the floor of the cage."

"Is this something you heard, or something you know?" JW asked.

"I've only been down a couple of times, but I'm in no hurry to go down again. The cage only takes you so far, then you still have to go on the rake to get to tunnel twelve."

"I'm good on the trap door for the next while," JW said, thinking he didn't want to go any deeper in the ground than where they were already working.

"And it's not much better on the return ride to the surface. That old cage ain't too steady," Patty said.

The rake started moving, and JW tried to put the cage out of his mind. He doubted he'd be long on the door. He knew he could end up anywhere the bosses put him. He'd been back almost two weeks and hadn't worked with Shawn McGuire yet, but he heard his voice further back on the rake and knew he'd be seeing him tonight. He wondered how the night could get any worse.

Chapter 16

The summer was passing quickly, and between working in the pit, hauling coal with Mickey, and haymaking, JW didn't have much time for Beth. She said she understood, but JW didn't want to jeopardize their relationship. He planned a trip to the movie theatre soon. He hadn't known what to say when Beth asked if he was looking forward to school starting in another month, because unless his father's health improved miraculously, JW believed he would miss the year.

Alfred was good to look after much of the day-to-day chores, which included feeding the chickens and gathering their eggs. He fed the animals but found milking the cow a little too difficult, as his hands cramped from the repetitive work.

JW pulled on his clothes and made very little noise as he descended the stairs.

"Breakfast's ready, John Wallace," his mother said. "What have you planned for the day, dear?"

JW started eating the second he sat in the chair. "Gonna check on the garden and see if the hay is ready to cut in the lower field. I don't have any coal to haul today, so I was thinking if I get through my chores quickly enough, I would head over to Beth's for a while."

"Sounds like a pretty full day."

"How's Da?"

"His strength is getting a little better every day, I think."

"Yeah, I noticed his hands don't seem to shake when he cuts his meat anymore. Is he sleeping?"

"Yes, but he was awake for much of the night. He finds it difficult sleeping at night after lying around most of the day. But he's up longer periods of the day, and he started taking little walks, so before you know it...."

JW looked at his mother. "I know, Ma. Tell Da I'll see him at suppertime." JW finished the last of his eggs and headed for the barn.

Spring had been a little dry, and JW had been concerned the garden would be difficult to keep watered. He had marvelled at the simple irrigation system Alfred put in place. He'd put pieces of boards together in a V shape angled between the rows of plants. Much of the watering could be done from the barn where the pump was. Fortunately, the dry spell had ended, but the irrigation system was a great backup.

When he stepped in the barn, he was surprised to see that Lightning's stall was clean and that Alfred was brushing him.

"Morning, Alfred. I have the day off, so I can take over. Thanks for all your help. Ma sent out your breakfast." Although two months had passed since his arrival, Alfred still preferred to keep to the work shed. JW walked there with him, carrying the food his mother had prepared for Alfred.

"I made something for you, JW."

JW smiled, wondering if perhaps he'd made him a whistle. His eyes opened wide when he saw the beautiful model schooner Alfred was holding out to him. JW had tried his hand at carving some ships that had ended up looking more like boats, but this one he was sure was perfectly carved to scale. "This is beautiful," JW said, sounding like an awe-struck ten-year-old.

"I saw some of the carvings in here that someone had done, and thought I would do one. Some of those were quite good. Although they're not quite to scale, the sculptor has potential."

"I was trying to give myself a model to follow so I could build a real one, but I know that's just another dream that costs too much."

"Much of what you need is in the forest where you get your firewood. It would take a lot of hard work to get the trees cut and planed, but the—"

"I'd still have to know what I was doing," JW said, interrupting. "It's one thing to carve out a pretty model, but to be able to make it into a ship or even a boat? It would take a lifetime to learn those skills. I think my schoolin' days are behind me and that the coal mine is my new classroom."

"Then I could teach you and make sure you keep it to scale."

JW held out the schooner. It really was beautiful. "I'm sure a real ship is a lot different than this."

"Yes," Alfred said, smiling. "Quite a bit bigger for one thing, and heavier too."

"Beth's father is building a schooner in Louisbourg. Have you ever—"

"That was my life's work, JW. I built ships in Louisbourg first, and then as my skills were no longer needed, I built fishing boats for those who sought my services. As time went on, I took to the simple tasks of carpentry and built barns and houses when asked."

"Would you show me how to build? Teach me?"

"Of course. I will teach you how to build a ship, but we will build a boat. We can add a small mast or two so that you can have a sail, but we will also have oars, just in case the winds are not blowing. When you have time, we will begin your studies. But now it's time for me to eat breakfast and for you to milk the cow."

—

"Hurry, boy. Open the door."

The familiar voice of Shawn McGuire echoed along the tunnel. JW came to the trap door that young Donnie was tending and saw how scared he looked as Shawn barked his orders.

"Hey, take it easy on him," JW said, and watched as Shawn stiffened and turned slowly toward him. His look of fear at being caught changed to one of embarrassment and then anger.

"Who do you think you are, boy, talking to me that way?"

"What way?"

"A little too big for your britches aren't you?"

"I hear you and some of the other men talking about how the company doesn't treat them right. Why should they, when some of you can't even treat other miners right?" JW moved closer to where Shawn McGuire stood. "He's just a young fella that doesn't want to be here. Why do you have to try to scare him? Isn't it miserable enough to be down here when you don't want to be? I know lots like the job. Some choose it, but some don't. Donnie didn't, so just let him be."

"That's pretty big talk. Your father ain't here to protect you," Shawn said, a sneer on his face.

"I don't need anyone to protect me. Don't you think it's time to stop picking on boys?" JW said. He was unaware that his father had had to have a talk with McGuire, telling him to go easy on the trapper boys. JW watched the smug look turn to one of hatred and realized he had gone too far.

"Ya got a smart mouth, boy," Shawn said, and slapped his horse to move him through the now open door.

There had been a time when Shawn had seemed kinder – above ground, at least – but JW had seen a change in him when he visited Mickey. Lately when JW entered the Mc-Guires' home, Shawn would leave the room, and then this summer not allowing Mickey to use the horse to haul coal with JW was further evidence that the man didn't care for him much.

"Thanks for sticking up for me, JW, but ain't he just gonna take it out on me when you're not around?" Donnie asked.

JW looked into Donnie's eyes and realized his mistake. Shawn would surely make a point of picking on Donnie as a way of getting back at JW. "You might be right. Sorry, Donnie. I was just trying to help."

"Yeah, I know. He hollers at me most nights anyway."

JW changed the subject. "How far did you go in school?"

"I finished grade seven and spent a month in grade eight, but it got too hard working the breakers and going to school. I liked it though, when I was there. Mrs. Johnson was nice," Donnie said.

"She was my favourite. Still is."

"Mine too."

"The thing you have to remember is not to let the other miners know what you're scared of. I don't much like the dark or walking by graveyards late at night, but I wouldn't tell anyone. Besides, you and I know there's no such thing as ghosts. The sounds we hear down here are just the wind. Just the wind," JW said, hoping to convince himself.

"I guess that's right, JW," Donnie said, but there was less conviction in his voice than JW's.

"Sure it is," JW said. "Well I gotta get to my trap before the trams head that way. Try not to worry about Shawn." JW followed a short distance behind Shawn McGuire, happy that he was in another area of the mine and that he wouldn't have to deal with him again tonight. He listened as some miners' voices echoed off the tunnel walls. *No wonder Donnie's afraid*, JW thought, and picked up his pace.

There was a spike in the wall in this new location where he was able to hang his satchel. He ate a sandwich down to the crust then flung the remaining pieces to the rats. JW's mind raced as he considered doing the same task day after day. He could make better money if he moved to tunnel twelve, and Mickey, now working there, had told him it wasn't too bad. The thought of the extra money weighed heavily, because JW knew his parents needed all they could get until his father was well enough to return to his job. *If he gets better*, JW thought. But when he thought of having to be dropped in a cage to the depths below, the trap job didn't seem so terrible. The sound of an approaching tram brought JW out of his ruminations, and he prepared to open the door.

Chapter 17

"Did you see that, Mary? He never even mentioned that today is the first day of school. I hate that he's missing the first week or possibly the first month, but I'm getting stronger every day. I should be back to work within the month," Andrew said.

"JW knows all too well that it's the first day, but I think he might be taking this year off," Mary answered. "He said even if you get back, he could work the year and save most of it toward college." Mary looked at her husband, and her heart ached for him. She knew he felt responsible for JW not being in school. "Remember I told him that grade eight was all he ever needed?" she said. "Well now he's got a grade eleven. And God knows that's more than he'll ever need living in this town."

"Yes, but he doesn't want to stay here. He wants to travel," Andrew said.

"He seems pretty content to travel the path to Beth's each day," Mary said.

Andrew chuckled.

"And maybe he'll do fine in the mine and stay there," Mary said. "He said that Alfred is going to teach him how to build a boat. Apparently that was what Alfred did in his earlier years."

"At least it will give him something to do on his days off. But Alfred could be gone any time."

"I think Alfred's content right where he is. He's like a grandfather for JW. Now all they need are some tools for carving and shaping the wood. I am so glad he's stayed. He's been a blessing to JW – and to us – and I think he likes to feel useful. JW said maybe he'll get his ship yet."

Andrew smiled sadly. "Yeah, he just might, more likely a boat, but perhaps something big enough to suit his needs. I think I'll pay Alfred a little visit. I just might sit in when he's teaching JW, to see if I can pick up a few tips."

"Sure, maybe build two ships and you can become pirates together," Mary said as she picked up the few breakfast dishes from the table. "If you need any more tips, I can show you how to wash the clothes and bake bread."

"That's just cruel, Mary," Andrew said, laughing, as he pulled the door closed behind him.

—

"Da is getting stronger every day, Beth, and he should be back to work shortly, but I've missed almost a month already. Won't be any catching up this year. I'm going to save what money I can and maybe go back next year. By then you'll be in nursing."

"I'm sorry you won't be back this year."

"Would you marry a miner, Beth? 'Cause that might be what I end up doing."

"You asked me this before, and I said not any miner, but I'd marry you even if you sold fish for a living."

"Well Alfred is going to teach me about boatbuilding, so maybe I will be a fisherman. He said that if we are able to start soon, we may have a good-sized boat ready come the spring. For now, though, I'm leaving the trap door and will be going deeper in the mine, down in tunnel twelve. Mickey's there now, and he said the money's better. If I'm going to be underground, I might as well earn the most I can."

"What does your father think?" Beth asked.

"I haven't told him yet, but it's not that I chose it anyway. The overman replacing Da told me he was putting me there. The size of me looks a little strange on the trap door when most of the boys doing the job are the size of Patty and Donnie." JW watched as Beth digested the information. He was surprised when her arms circled his waist, and more surprised when she laid her head against his chest and fell silent.

"What's wrong, Beth? Are you okay?"

"You just told me you won't be back to school this year, and then you tell me you're going deeper into the mine, where I'm sure it's a lot more dangerous. That's what's wrong. I'm worried for you."

JW took a deep breath and tried to reassure her. "I'm not worried about it. I'm quite sure it's almost as safe as being on the trap door, only a little deeper, that's all," JW said, wishing he believed what he was saying.

"But you'll be careful, right, JW?" Beth said.

"Oh, I'll be extra careful. Can't afford to get injured, or Davey Brown will be sweet-talking you again."

"No, I think he knows that there's only one boy for me, JW, and it's you. But he is kinda handsome." She laughed at the look on JW's face. "Just kidding," she said.

JW took her hands in his and hugged her to him.

—

"Well, our coal hauling is pretty much done for this year," JW said.

"Why's that?" Andrew asked.

"I've gotta cut the last of the hay and then get it in the barn. I don't want to wear out poor old Lightning. Besides, I need some time to do other things."

"Wouldn't have anything to do with a certain pretty girl that lives in a hollow, would it?" his mother called from the kitchen.

JW laughed. "I can't fool you, can I, Ma?"

Mary laughed too.

"The trap door's only givin' you three or so shifts a week, so you should be able to squeeze a few loads of coal in, if you and Mickey are on the same shift," his father said.

JW looked at his father and knew what he said next would upset him, but better for his father to hear it from him than from someone else. "I'm not going to be on the trap much longer, maybe another day or so."

"What?"

"I'm going to tunnel twelve, starting next week. Mickey's already there."

"I wish you'd discussed it with me before deciding to follow your buddy deeper into the mine."

"I didn't ask for it. Anderson told me I was too big to be on a trap door and that he was moving me down below."

Andrew Donaldson looked at his son. So much had changed in the last three years. As big as he was, he was still a boy with dreams. If he squealed the first night going down on the trip, Andrew was worried he could have the same or worse response his first time going down in the cage. "Well Anderson had no business saying that. I'll go in and see—"

"It's bad enough having to work with Shawn, but if you do that, everyone would be laughing at me. I gotta do it."

Andrew sighed deeply and lowered his voice. "Yes, you're right, but it's not easy work, and the new guys are always given a rough time at first. It'd be good if you and Mickey were together on the same shift."

"Yeah, someone to travel with."

"It's hard, dangerous work. Pick and shovel, and there'll be a lot of blasting as they move the tunnel deeper."

JW saw the look of concern, and the realization of what he would be facing started to set in. He began to say something, but his father spoke first.

"I'm not trying to scare you, but this is real mining, and you should have a healthy fear of what you'll be facing. This is where even experienced miners sometimes get seriously hurt, or worse, so you have to have eyes in the back of your head to keep safe. I wanted you to learn the ropes, spend some more time on the trap door, do some coal hauling ... stuff like that."

"I'll be careful, Da. I remember what you taught me from before."

"Did he say what you'd be doing?"

"No, he just said, 'No more trap doors for you. You're going to tunnel twelve.' It sounded like a punishment. I never did anything wrong, and I never spoke more than two words to the man."

"I know who he is, but I don't know much about him, and I can't remember ever working with him."

"Sounds like it'll be more hours and better pay."

"Yes to both, but you'll earn every penny of it. We were having some issues with twelve before I got sick. I don't know if there've been more problems since."

"Mickey hasn't said anything, but Patty might know."

"Patty does seem to know everything that's going on," Andrew said, and smiled. "I just wish I hadn't told your mother about all the issues with twelve. She'll be beside herself with worry, once she knows."

"Knows what?" Mary said, coming into the dining room.

The deafening silence seemed to last minutes, as JW and his father exchanged glances.

"JW's going down tunnel twelve, starting next week," Andrew said, and watched as the news sunk in.

"Tunnel twelve? Tunnel twelve! You said you were scared down there. There's no way he's going down there," Mary said, speaking as if JW wasn't in the room. "You'll just have to go and tell them, Andy. He can't go there, he just can't." She put her hands up to hide her tears and hurried from the room.

JW and his father sat there, heavy-hearted, as they heard the outside door open and close.

Chapter 18

JW watched Tennyson walk toward him, his limp pronounced, as if the rainy weather was affecting him. JW laid his palm on the barn's floor, and Tennyson crawled up and settled into the crook of his arm. His old friend took his time eating the oats from JW's other hand. The whiskers on his face seemed whiter than even a few weeks ago.

Alfred entered the room, depending heavily on his walking stick. In his other arm, Beauty rested against his chest. Alfred laid his walking stick down, limped to the workbench and made a place for Beauty to watch him as he worked. He hadn't noticed JW and Tennyson.

JW scratched the head of his pet rat and was struck by the similarity of white whiskers on both Tennyson and Alfred, and they both limped. Not for the first time he felt a pang of regret for the injury he had caused to Tennyson, and he petted him again. He smiled. The old man, Alfred, and JW's pet rat, Tennyson, together made the name Alfred, Lord Tennyson – his favourite poet.

"Perhaps it's time we introduce Tennyson and Beauty to each other, since they have to share the space," JW called across the room.

"Goodness! I didn't see you there, JW," Alfred said. "Yes, let us see how two naturally sworn enemies react."

JW knew that Beauty would grow to be four or five times the size of Tennyson. But for now, although Beauty was close to twice his size, he gave the edge to Tennyson for his wily ways.

JW walked closer to Beauty, and he felt Tennyson bristle, pushing against his arm as he struggled to get down. Beauty's diet of cow's milk meant she hadn't considered other sources of food. She made no effort to strike out at Tennyson. JW knew she was still very young, which was why he thought there was time to have them, if not become friends, at least coexist. JW stayed close by as he laid Tennyson on the bench next to Beauty. He thought it might have been pride that kept Tennyson from scurrying from the bench when Beauty approached.

JW hoped they would at least get along as well as Gulliver and Tennyson did. Those two had forged a grudging tolerance of each other. Beauty's outstretched paw was met with a small nip of Tennyson's teeth, but neither seemed ready to attack. After several minutes of watching their limited interaction, JW decided it was time to separate the two. He petted Tennyson's head and lowered him to the floor.

"If you have time, I could show you what tools are needed to build your boat," Alfred said. "I have some, and your grandfather's shed has others that we will need. They are old but well-oiled and are of high quality. But we will need several more, some bigger planes to hew the bigger planks. They may be costly, but perhaps there is someone from whom you can borrow?"

"I don't know anyone who has boat-building tools, who isn't using them," JW said. "And I'm not sure they would be willing to lend them if I did. Guess that puts an end to our plans to build a boat."

"Unless we make our own," Andrew Donaldson said.

JW and Alfred turned to where Andrew now stood.

"Your grandfather was a pretty good blacksmith, and he taught me the trade before I went to the pit. There is still a forge we can use."

"You mean you can make the tools we might need, Da?"

"Well, more like I can show you how to make the tools you'll need. I'll get you started. When my strength comes back, I'll help a little more, but for now, you can swing the hammer to flatten out the iron."

"Shipbuilding and blacksmithing skills! I won't need to go back to school, and I might even be able to get out of the coal mines," JW said, laughing. "Just hope I can learn well enough to build more than a raft."

"Between your father and me, we will have you working in both crafts very soon. Then after years of practice you will master them. But like the alphabet, you have to learn A before B," Alfred said. Looking around, he added, "This barn is very big. You could build the boat within its walls, if your father permits."

"That would be best to keep everything as dry as possible," Andrew said. "Besides, there is more than enough room for the animals."

"Thanks, Da. That's great," JW said.

Andrew looked over his shoulder as he was leaving the barn and smiled at the animated conversation going on between the old man and his son. He caught JW's eye and winked at him, getting a smile in return.

JW made a clucking sound and Lightning moved forward. He knew pulling the hay cutter through the thick grass in the fields was hard on the old horse but was surprised at the pace at which he moved. The usual scraping sound from the wheels was gone, and he realized the seat was no longer lopsided. JW stopped and got off the cutter. He saw that the wheels had been greased and the seat straightened and, more importantly, the blades had been sharpened. Climbing back into the seat, he got back to cutting the field and finished hours earlier than usual. The only pauses were to give Lightning a rest and some oats and water. The chore done, now the hay would lie in the field and dry before he would again harness Lightning, when it was time to rake.

JW smiled when he pulled the barn door open and it swung easily outward then closed gently behind him and Lightning. He brushed down the horse and brought more water and oats then went looking for Alfred. JW found him reading in the shed.

"You've been busy," JW said. "The cutter moves like a fish through water, and the door moves like.... Thank you."

"I saw something where I could help, and I did. I'm glad it made things easier for you and Lightning," Alfred said.

Chapter 19

JW saw the flickering light coming toward him. If it was one of the old open-flame headlamps moving that fast, he was sure it would go out. There was a muffled sound of crying in the air. His heart went out to the boy who stood before him, shoulders shaking as he tried not to sob.

"I'm scared, JW. I saw someone – something – coming down the tunnel calling my name," Donnie said. "I just wanna go home." Donnie looked at the floor.

JW knew Donnie was embarrassed, but the fear he felt overrode the embarrassment. Putting his hand on Donnie's shoulder, he tried to reassure him. "It's okay to be afraid, but you can't let it make you panic." JW quickly added, "I've panicked a time or two, but you can be fired for leaving the trap door."

"But it was calling my name, JW," Donnie said, calmer now that he was no longer alone.

"Remember we talked about how it's only the wind?"

"Yeah—"

"Well, that's all it was, 'cause there's no such thing as ghosts."

"They told me," Donnie said, referring to the older miners, "about the men who'd been killed 'cause of the boys who'd fallen asleep. They said they'd come to get us in the night."

"Even if that was true," JW said, and saw Donnie's eyes open wide, "which it's not, you never fell asleep and had men die because of it, have you?"

"No, I'm too afraid to sleep," Donnie said.

"Well then, why would ghosts be after you? And the wind howling or the dead silence can make you think you're hearing things," JW said, hoping Donnie believed him.

"Yeah, I guess," Donnie said, not sounding totally convinced but less afraid.

"We'd better get you back to your door before a tram comes along. C'mon."

The walk back to his door only took a few minutes. When it came into view, Donnie picked up his pace and called "Thank you" in the darkness. JW would soon be leaving for tunnel twelve, but he didn't have the heart to tell Donnie, who would have only Patty left to stick up for him.

—

Mickey looked into Sally's eyes. He liked that she held his hand tightly. They talked a lot about the future. Pretty much every time they saw each other they discussed marriage and the number of children they would have some day. Sally's plans included finishing high school and becoming a nurse. She'd told Mickey that she and Beth would do the program together.

"Sally," Mickey said, his voice displaying the nervousness he felt.

Sally looked into his eyes. "Yes, Mickey?"

"You know I like— love you, right?"

"I think so."

"Well, I don't think we should wait another two or three years to get married."

"But, Mickey, I still have a lot of schoolin' ahead of me."

"You won't need any more school once we're married," Mickey said.

"But where would we live? And how would we afford all the things we need?"

"I don't have all the answers, but it'll work out somehow. I'm working tunnel twelve now, and the money's better, so that should do. That's all Da has coming in, and we all manage just fine," Mickey said, not bothering to add that he and his family had missed more than a few meals over the years, or that most of his pay went to help feed his little brother and sisters.

"But where would we live? There's no room at your place or mine," Sally said.

Mickey wanted so badly to be out of his house, he'd be willing to live in a barn if he had to. He hadn't considered that he and Sally might have to live with family. The thought of them living with his parents made him reconsider. "You're right, there is no room. I guess I never thought of all we'd need. And if we're both working we'd have more money, at least until the babies came along." He didn't see the relieved look on Sally's face at the reprieve she'd been given.

"Yes, and the time will fly by quickly, and then we'll be married with a place of our own," Sally said. "I'd better get along home. Ma needs some help with the little ones."

Mickey walked her to her door then went back the way he'd come, passing by his grandfather's house. His mother's father was a kind, gentle man with hands the size of pan shovels, the kind used to load coal. He had worked the mines and didn't have a problem with his oldest daughter marrying a miner, not until she'd been a few months into the marriage and he'd gotten to see the true colours of Shawn McGuire – mean to the core. He'd told his daughter that she could return home anytime she wished, but he knew she never would.

Mickey turned and looked at the large house that his grandfather lived in all alone and decided to pay him a visit. He tried to drop by as often as he could to spend time with him, but with work and the coal hauling he and JW had been doing, he hadn't seen him for almost a month. The door to the house opened as he pushed through the gate on the fence.

"I saw you walking by and hoped you might have time for a little visit," his grandfather said, opening the door wider as Mickey started to enter.

"Sorry I haven't been by much lately, Grandpa. Me and JW were hauling coal after work, so I didn't have much time."

"Yes, and I see you're still spending time with Amos's daughter. Before long you'll be old and married with kids of your own."

Mickey looked around the room, taking in the photographs of his grandmother and those of his own mother and her sisters. There had been no boys before Mickey, so he was held in high regard by his grandfather. Oh, Mickey knew that his grandfather loved his granddaughters and grandsons equally and that he tried not to show any favouritism, but it would be to him and his little brother he would tell the stories of his time in the mines.

"Sally and I were just talking about getting married but think we should wait until we have a place to live. She plans to be a nurse," Mickey told his grandfather.

"Waiting would probably be best. With the mines the way they are these days, another strike or closure could happen anytime. Come to think of it, that's the way they've always been and probably always will be, so I guess you can't wait forever."

"Grandpa, me and Da aren't getting along too good these days. Ha! Can't remember when we ever did." Mickey looked around the room, delaying what he wanted to ask, trying to summon up the courage. "I was wondering if I could move in with you. I wouldn't be any trouble, and I'd give you whatever you needed out of my pay to help with groceries and such." Mickey held his breath, waiting for his grandfather's response.

"You'd be more than welcome to stay with me, but I wouldn't want to cause any trouble for your mother. Like you, I don't get along too well with your father, and I can't remember when we ever did. I don't like to speak ill of your father, but he's a bully, picking on those most likely to be afraid of him, so I would want you to talk it over with your mother first. If it's okay with her, you can come here as soon as you want."

"Thanks, Grandpa. I'll talk to Ma tonight after Da goes to work. I best get home for supper. Talk to you later."

As he closed the gate behind him, Mickey started to realize that his leaving would cause trouble for his mother in more than one way. She'd lose his money coming in, and she'd have to listen to his father growling about his leaving. He was conflicted by his desire to get out of the house away from his father and not wanting to make it any harder on his mother than it already was.

The sun was shining, but the cool air sent a chill across his shoulders. His path toward adulthood had a lot of hills and valleys, and seemed destined to unfold however it would. By the time he opened the door to his house, Mickey knew he would not ask his mother tonight. He would wait a while longer. At least he knew he could stay with his grandfather. He sighed deeply as his foot crossed the threshold.

Chapter 20

JW looked at the huge bull wheel, which looked like a Ferris wheel with no seats. It was used to hoist the cage that he and the other miners would be in. The cage would drop vertically more than eight hundred feet. The rake going down the slope at high speeds didn't compare to this. His father had explained the difference between slope mining and vertical mining before, but it had only been in passing. Over the weekend, his father had told him about the bull wheels that raised and lowered the cage by using cables, made of wire braided like rope. There was a man driving an engine that controlled the speed of the descent and ascent. JW had learned that the lowering and raising both happened at about the same speed. His father said the cage was supposed to go slower when the men travelled to and from the mine and faster when it was just the coal being raised. But the owners were always after more and more production and wanted the cage moving as fast as it could go every time.

"This doesn't feel like a fast train ride, JW," his father said. "Even after you get used to it, and many never do, most times it feels as if your stomach is still topside. Shaft mining or vertical mining uses a cage to get the men, materials, coal and horses in and out of the mine. It's like the elevator in that department store in North Sydney, but there's no door. Only a bar across the opening keeps the men in."

JW had sat quietly taking it all in. This wasn't a story to explain the importance about staying awake on the trap door. This was to let him know it was going to be really scary.

"Sometimes you have to travel on another rake to get you to where you'll be working, JW, and that's the case in tunnel twelve. Straight down a long way, and then down the slope for quite aways. I'm not trying to scare you, just prepare you, because the usual bunch will be trying to put fear in you. You're gonna hear about broken cables on the cage and how dangerous it is. And it's all true. If the cable breaks, you better hope the cage is near the bottom, because, if not, it's serious injury – or worse." JW noticed his father hadn't used the word death, but he figured it was all too real a possibility.

JW walked over to the shaft and peered down into an abyss. Looking straight up, he noticed the cables were moving, and he backed away from the edge. A few moments later he saw the cage break the surface. Some of the men exiting the cage looked pale, as if they'd been out on a rough sea. Others didn't seem to mind it, and he hoped he could be more like them.

"Hey, JW," Mickey called.

"Hiya, Mickey."

"Looking to make some better money?"

"Apparently Anderson thinks I must want it, because he volunteered me."

"Look at the bright side; at least you won't have to see Da on any of your shifts. He's scared to death of the cage. Cable broke on a shift right before his a few years back, and he never worked that shift or any others that required a cage to get below. Four men and two horses were killed. There were no survivors."

Mickey paused, and the two looked at each other, wordless for a moment.

"Da didn't seem too pleased when he heard I was coming here," JW said, "and Ma is beside herself with worry. She wanted Da to go and get me outta working tunnel twelve. But he and I both know I got no choice for now."

"Ma doesn't know that I've moved from the trap. Da does. He's not saying much, but I guess he's worried too. We're not really seeing eye-to-eye these days. I asked Grandpa if I could move in with him."

"What did he say?"

"He said as long as it doesn't cause any trouble for Ma. Grandpa is not too impressed with the old fella either, but he doesn't want any more misery for Ma. I thought about it on the walk home, and I realized that Ma needs the money I'm bringing in. It'll be at least another year before Greg can start in the mines. Poor fella, I don't think he knows he's next on the list to work in the pit," Mickey said.

"Well, Da's starting to get his strength back, so he could be back in a month or two," JW said.

"That's great news. Does that mean back to school for you then?" Mickey asked.

"Not this year. I've missed too much time. I didn't think Da would ever be going back to work, so I never even went the first day, and it's over a month since school started. But Alfred will be teaching me how to build a boat, and Da is going to be showing me some blacksmithing skills. If we're going to be on the same shift, you could come over and learn with me."

"I'm sure there would be a lot of arithmetic needed to build a boat," Mickey said.

"There's a fair bit, I'm sure, but most of it should be hands-on, same with the blacksmith stuff. Be nice to have a boat to do some fishing on our days off. You can still be the first mate."

They both laughed. JW saw the men making their way to the cage, and Mickey motioned for him to head toward it. "Remember to keep your eyes closed. It's like when we jump off the cliff swimming, except it seems to last forever instead of a few seconds. Just don't scream here, even if you have to bite your tongue."

"Ain't gonna happen," JW said, hoping he could keep his word. Squaring his shoulders, he stepped into the cage. He looked at the other men. No one seemed in the mood to tease anyone. Everyone seemed to be lost in their thoughts. Maybe they are readying themselves for the descent, JW thought. He watched the lips of some of the miners; they seemed to be praying. Disorientation overtook him as the cage dropped.

—

Beth looked out her bedroom window. She knew worrying for JW was futile, because he would have to face danger every time he entered the pit. If only the kids at school hadn't told her about tunnel twelve and the dangers it posed. JW had told her of his first night going down on the trip; how he'd let out a scream as it plummeted down the slope. He'd only been thirteen, thrust into an adult world. Beth figured he might still be afraid but doubted now, at sixteen, he'd let others see.

She missed walking to school with JW, talking about their future. Although she was proud he was doing the right thing, helping out his family, she truly wished he could just be there with her. She pulled the blankets down and slid beneath the cool sheets, sighing deeply as she thought about his first night going down that shaft. Despite her worrying, she felt the arms of sleep enfold her, and she smiled as JW's face came to mind.

Chapter 21

"Holy gee, Mickey. I thought I was gonna lose my supper," JW said, his legs shaky from the cage ride. "I don't know if I'll ever get used to dropping like that, especially with my eyes closed. There seemed to be a little whimpering going on. Was that you?"

"Wasn't me. Some of the men hate this more than me, but they gotta feed their families. Can you imagine, being afraid every day before you even start work and then having to do it all over again the next day, for forty years?"

Feelings of dread and despair came over JW, but he pushed them away. *No one to come rescue me from it all. This just might have to be my life's work*, JW thought. "Not what I want to do, Mickey, but if I have to, I will. But I'll try to get a job where I won't be dropping over eight hundred feet every day."

"Don't forget there is still the ride on the rake another mile or so before we start work. If you find one of those jobs, I'd like one too."

The ride on the rake seemed a snail's pace compared to the cage. As it came to a stop, JW heard an explosion.

"Yep, that's where we're going, JW. Maimed and dead are two real possibilities, so keep your eyes open. You watch my back, and I'll watch yours."

JW nodded, and they walked in silence as he took in his surroundings. The coal dust lay like a heavy morning fog, the helmet lamp barely casting enough light to see where they were going. Dust soon found its way into their mouths, noses and lungs. JW licked his lips and quickly spat. As he closed his mouth his teeth felt gritty, and he spat again but soon realized that his mouth would just get dried out, and he still would have the same gritty feeling on his teeth and tongue. Reluctantly, he swallowed the coal dust mixing with his saliva.

Reaching the work area, he saw that there was little explanation required. His father said there would be blasting, shovelling and a fair bit of pick use. The mine was almost as high as he was tall, which provided some relief. He might have to bend over slightly, but if he widened his stance, his head didn't quite reach the ceiling. He was glad that he and Mickey would be working together.

"You're Andy's boy, ain't you?" one of the miners asked.

"Yes, sir, I am."

"Name's Butts, and this is Dawe. We both worked with and for your father. He's a good man, and he sure is missed. Hope he's gettin' along good."

"Yeah, he's getting better every day," JW said. "He figures he could be back in a month or two," he added.

"That's good news. When he replaced Red, things got even better than under Red, and Red was a real good man too," Butts said.

"We just did a blast," Dawe said. "More than enough to last you the shift. You'll spend your shift with your head down, shovelling. Say hi to Andy."

"Be extra careful, boys. There was another roof collapse today," Butts said.

"Yeah, almost a daily occurrence," Dawe added.

JW watched as the two older miners headed back the way he and Mickey had come. One was walking with a limp, but it didn't seem to slow him down. JW remembered what his father had said about tunnel twelve. "You have to have eyes in the back of your head to keep safe." He heard the clang of metal on metal and turned to see Mickey getting ready to load the tram. JW hurried to pick up a shovel. The summer spent hauling coal together was evident as they fell into a rhythm, matching shovelful for shovelful, quickly filling the tram.

They watched as the small Sable Island horse strained to get the tram moving. The first few feet splayed the horse's legs so much it looked as if they would break under the tremendous strain, but once it got started, it appeared effortless for the little horse. Moments later, the next tram was in place, ready to be filled.

"Not much time in between," JW said.

"It keeps up like this all night," Mickey said.

Some of the pieces were too big for the shovel and had to be thrown in the tram by hand; others were so large they had to be broken apart with the pick.

"Well at least I won't fall asleep, but I don't guess we'll get any time for treasure hunting."

"No treasure hunting, unless they get backed up at the cage. But you'll sleep like a baby when you get home in the morning," Mickey said.

Not having been around many babies, JW hoped that meant they slept well. "I still have a lot of harvesting to do. Potatoes, turnips and some other stuff still need to be pulled and stored for the winter, and I have to finish cutting up the wood."

"This ain't the trap door, JW. You won't be able to shovel coal all night and work half the day in the fields and woods. It's steady work, mostly every night or day. All you're gonna want to do is sleep when you get home. We're off in a few days. I can help you then," Mickey said.

"Thanks, Mickey. I guess I'll know in the morning if I can get anything done," JW said, as the next tram stopped and he and Mickey started shovelling again.

It was difficult to carry on a conversation, because the noise of the shovels drowned out their voices and JW spoke through mostly clenched teeth; he didn't want to eat anymore coal dust than he had to.

The night passed quickly, but by morning JW was so tired his arms and legs felt like he'd been drawn and quartered. After some thought, he supposed being pulled apart by horses would have been much worse. The ride to the surface was just as quick as the descent, and he didn't have to be told to close his eyes. They were closing on their own. The coursing water from the shower seemed to bring a little relief to his tired muscles as he washed the coal dust from his body. He couldn't imagine trying to pull vegetables this morning. He coughed and spat up dust that had tried to find a permanent home in his throat and lungs.

That was his first night of working as a coal miner, and he thought of his father who'd spent more than twenty years doing this very work. JW shuddered. *Is this what I've signed up for, for the rest of my life?* He pushed the thought away.

JW dressed quickly and picked up his satchel, brushing the coal dust from it and remembering that Grandpa Donaldson had told him it had many compartments where he could hide his secrets. Tennyson was one such secret, when JW took him out of the mine hidden inside. JW wished it held the secret of his future.

JW's legs felt rubbery as he started his walk homeward. Being bent in a squat position most of the shift, shovelling, had caused his legs to cramp, and now they just wanted to rest. He was never so happy to see his house. Gulliver bounded along the pathway toward him, but he was too tired to bend down and pet him. Instead, Gulliver jumped up and JW petted him, cooing some words to his best friend. "Atta boy, Gullie. Good to see you too, boy," JW said, eyeing the entrance to his house. All he wanted was sleep.

"Will you have time for a lesson today, JW?" Alfred called to him as he neared the house.

"No, not today, Alfred. I'm so tired I can barely keep my eyes open. I never realized how difficult the work in the mines was until last night. Now I know why my father is so strong."

"Perhaps we'll get to it once you have a day off."

"I wish, but I have fields to harvest and wood to cut. I think it may have to wait until I get all my other work done. But I'm really looking forward to it," he quickly added.

"Another time, JW. Sleep well," Alfred said, and walked toward the barn.

As JW reached for the door latch, he remembered the cow needed to be milked and fed, and the other chores for Lightning and the chickens had to be done. There weren't enough hours in the day. His lumbering steps somehow propelled him to the barn, and he pulled the pail from the shelf and washed it free of dust before sitting to milk the cow. Leaning his head against the cow's side, JW almost fell asleep during the milking.

He put the full milk bucket back on the shelf and started cleaning the stalls of both Lightning and the cow, the muscles in his arms screaming in protest. There was an abundance of eggs this morning, and JW didn't want to make a second trip. He was glad when Alfred offered to collect them for him. He was surprised and pleased to see Beauty and Tennyson sharing space. Not counting the hens and cow, Beauty was the only female in the barn.

"Nice to see them getting along," JW said.

"I have been bringing Beauty in here several times a day, and Tennyson has started to accept her. But I think she will soon be queen of all she sees. Even Gulliver is good with her. He just sniffs her and moves on. They are not, perhaps, best friends, but they are learning to tolerate each other. Too bad the rest of the world couldn't get along so well."

"Peace is a wonderful idea, but right now, sleep seems as important. Thanks for gathering the eggs, Alfred," JW said. "I've got to get in the house now, or I may fall asleep in the barn."

JW placed the milk on the kitchen table, said good morning and goodnight to his parents, then slowly took the stairs one at a time. His eyes closed before his head hit the pillow.

Chapter 22

Taking in her surroundings, Beth inhaled the strong antiseptic smell deeply into her lungs. The sterile atmosphere made her catch her breath.

"Hurry on, Beth. We have to get to Mr. Smith. He needs his bath."

"Coming, Sister," Beth said. Although she knew some of the nuns' names, calling them all Sister was easier. She was excited when she'd found out she'd been accepted into the nursing program and pleased it was nearby, at Hamilton Memorial Hospital in North Sydney. Both she and Sally had been notified at the same time, and neither had had the chance to tell JW or Mickey yet. She was more than happy to leave grade twelve to start training for her career.

They were in the classroom each day, but they also spent time with patients. If she had the notion that her days would be passed simply sitting next to patients holding their hands, telling them all would be well, it was quickly changed. Bedpans and chamber pots needed to be emptied and cleaned, and baths had to be given.

Beth and Sally saw little of each other the first few days, passing quickly in the hallways. Between classroom work and time spent with patients, Beth found there was a lot to learn. Once she was a nurse, she knew she would have to work different shifts: day time as well as overnight. With JW working shifts as well, they could go extended periods without seeing each other. She pushed the thought from her mind. It will work itself out, she thought.

The hospital ward was large, and some of the people were old and feeble. She wanted to reassure them and read to them but knew that practical stuff came first. She pulled the curtains around Mr. Smith's bed, like she'd been shown by the Sister. She drew the water in the basin and stood back as the nun prepared to show her how to do the bath. She thought it would be quite easy, but the logistics were important, because they dealt with the dignity of the patient. Beth blushed at the thought of having to bathe the adults and guessed that was why the Sister's attitude was very businesslike in her explanation and carrying out of the chore – maybe she too was embarrassed.

Mr. Smith was old and, Beth learned, near death, and that was why they had to bathe him. He no longer had the strength to care for himself. In school, Beth had learned of Florence Nightingale, the nurse who'd been responsible for improving hospital conditions. She'd read that Florence had spent countless hours consoling the patients, making her rounds late at night, carrying a lamp, checking on the ill. She'd become known as the Lady of the Lamp. She was a big influence on Beth's decision to become a nurse. Beth had dreamed of caring for the sick by comforting them, almost forgetting that Florence was responsible for major changes in hygiene, which led to a huge reduction in infections.

"Good morning, Mr. Smith," the Sister said.

Beth watched the old man smile, and she added, "Good morning, sir" and received a smile and a nod.

"Beth and I are going to freshen you up and change your bedding. We'll try to get it done quickly."

Beth saw the old man smile again and thought he must not have the strength to answer. His breakfast tray on the bedside table seemed to be untouched, except for perhaps a few sips of tea and a small piece of toast. Once the bath was done and the bedding changed, Beth thought Mr. Smith looked more comfortable. She bundled the clothes and took them to be laundered. Along the way, she heard a hacking cough coming from a room and peeked in. She listened to the doctor say matter-of-factly, "Forty years of breathing coal dust is what's wrong, Bill. You should come out of the mines to give your lungs a chance to clear out a little."

"Ain't no jobs on the top for me, doctor. Even the breaker boys are breathing in the dust all day. I never went but a few years in school, and what little I learnt is long forgotten. I gotta feed me and the family. How much do I owe ya?"

"Nothing, Bill. It already comes off your cheque. Try to get some fresh air when you can."

Beth moved away from the door before the doctor and patient came out, her thoughts on JW. She worried what a lifetime underground would mean for him. She said a little prayer that he would be safe, then hurried to the laundry. There was much more to do before her shift was over. She was glad that she was only a half-hour walk from home.

She and Sally could make the walk together. The Sisters had told them that during stormy days, they could stay in the dormitory at the hospital. Beth didn't like the thought of overnights at the hospital but was glad it was an option, just one she hoped she wouldn't have to use. She glanced out the window overlooking Sydney Harbour and knew that was where JW would rather be – on the water. It seemed their summers of picnics, reading books and swimming were a thing of the past, as adult life made its presence felt.

Chapter 23

"Ma, Beth's been in nursing school for the past week. She and Sally," JW said, as he closed the kitchen door. "I just spent an hour with her."

"I know, dear. Her mother told me earlier today. Ain't that grand? She'll make a fine one too. So will Sally, I'm sure."

"It's like we're living in two different countries, instead of a mile apart. With working and sleeping...." Changing the subject, JW asked, "How's Da?"

"He's a lot better. He's out working with Alfred – said he's feeling stronger every day."

"That's good. I'll check in on them after I have a quick bite to eat. I'm glad for Beth. It's just that it took almost a week for me to find out. I guess times are changing."

Mary looked at JW and thought how serious and old he seemed. The hard work in the mines was showing on him, but she never heard him complain. She was glad that Andrew was able to start doing some of the chores again, and she'd surprised JW by milking the cow on several mornings before he got home.

—

JW watched as his father swung the hammer, sweat glistening on his forehead. This was the healthiest JW had seen his father in months. The ring of the hammer hitting the metal filled the small forge area. There was a loud hiss as the heated iron was dropped into a bucket of water. JW saw the skill with which his father handled the tongs to move another piece of glowing orange metal to the anvil. The hammer struck again; this time there was only a thudding sound as the piece of iron began to spread outward with each strike. As the glow started to fade, his father put it back in the fire. JW realized that if the iron was much hotter, it would be liquefied.

"Don't overdo it, Da, and tire yourself out," JW said, from behind him. He noticed his father didn't flinch.

Turning to face him, Andrew smiled. "It's the first time I've felt energetic for a while, and the work has given me an appetite." He showed JW his belt. "It's out a full notch, and after supper tonight, it might need to go out another."

Although his father was still slim, JW noticed his weight gain. It filled out the hollows in his cheeks, giving his face a healthier look. "What are you making?"

"The one in the pail will be used as a rough plane to cut through the knots in the wood, and this next piece will be for some of the finer work. Some of the others you'll need, I'll do once Alfred gets back."

"Back from where?" JW asked, noticing Beauty was wandering around the floor, pushing some straw about and jumping at any flies that came near.

"He said he had to see someone and would be back sometime tomorrow. That's all I know."

"I hope he's still going to teach me to build a ship— boat. I haven't had much time yet 'cause of the work in tunnel twelve, but I'm getting used to it, so I'm not as tired as I was," JW said.

"Don't worry, JW, he's waiting for you. He said he's going to teach you how to build both, but together you will try to finish a boat over the winter. He's been sharpening any of the tools I've made and laying out his own. He'll be ready to go once you are." Andrew paused. "Your mother told me Beth is in nursing. You two are all grown up." He smiled as JW picked up Tennyson from the floor. *Not quite*, he thought.

"Beth said the nursing has a lot more to it than she thought going in, but she says she likes it. I guess most jobs are like that. Once she's a nurse, she'll have to work shifts too, so when we're married, if we're on different shifts, we might not see each other for a week or more." JW stammered once he realized what he'd said. "I mean, if we were married." He continued to try to explain and then noticed his father was grinning at him.

"Where ya gonna live? Maybe you can build a boathouse and live in that. Be good in the summer, at least when the weather's good. Don't know about the winter though, once the ice comes."

"Good idea, Da," JW said, playing along, "but I'm not ready to give up Ma's cooking yet. Leastways, not until I'm sure Beth can cook almost as good," he said, rubbing his stomach.

"Since you're here, and it's too dark out to do anything else, you might as well try swinging the hammer a little to get used to the feel. I'll explain as we go. It's all about shaping the metal the way you want it. It's more involved, but it's sorta like the pick. You gotta strike the iron in certain places to get it to do what you want it to, just like swinging the pick and hitting the right spot to make the coal drop."

JW picked up the tongs and tried to pull the piece of iron from the forge. After several attempts, he started to get the hang of it. He let his father have the tongs and watched as he swung the hammer.

"The first swings are hard ones, then you gotta swing easier to get the metal to do its magic. This isn't all about brute strength, a lot of it's technique. You need to know where to hit and how hard, especially with some of the smaller tools Alfred said you're gonna need. So with this piece, watch how hard I hit it."

JW saw how the weight of the hammer falling on the hot metal spread it out. Taking the tongs and hammer, he tried to copy his father's swing but could tell his first swing was too hard, the small piece flattened more than when his father had struck it.

Andrew stepped closer to examine the slowly forming tool. "It's okay. Swing about half that weight this time, then I'll show you how to shape it."

JW did as his father told him, and they spent the next half-hour shaping the tool as twilight turned to dark.

—

Alfred breathed in the smell of the forest all around him, the pleasant and the not so pleasant odours, each telling their story. The oak and ash and bird's-eye maple were some of the wood he would teach JW about. Alfred was as silent in the woods as many of his mother's people were – each footstep carefully placed. Although he did not like killing animals, Alfred was a skilled hunter, only taking what was needed. Having spent so much time on or around the water, he preferred fish to meat but ate both.

His mother had been Mi'kmaq as had been his beloved Jenean. He had grown up learning to respect the earth and all it had to offer, to use only what he needed so that there would always be some left for those that came after. And to give thanks, always give thanks. From his father, he had learned the ways of the Europeans, and, although he was happier living from the land, he was glad he'd learned from his father. The skills to carve wood into useful things had become his life's work. As he walked along, he envisioned what some of the trees could become.

Alfred smelled the wood fire up ahead and called out. "Kwe." The greeting was quickly returned, and Alfred saw one of his nephews, Daniel, coming through the forest toward him. "Kwe, nklamuksis," Daniel said in greeting, calling him my uncle. They embraced, and Alfred walked with him to where he was camped. He would stay there this night and head back in the morning.

Chapter 24

JW hurried toward home. Day shifts started at seven, and it was close to five o'clock by the time he got home. The leaves on the trees had mostly all changed. The green of summer replaced by red, orange and yellow and various shades of those colours, with some of the leaves already lying on the ground, brown and withered.

There was evidence of frost this morning, and a chill in the air this afternoon. His mind raced, considering the potatoes and turnips still in the ground. If they were going to have any surplus, he had to get them out in the next few days even if it meant working in the dark. At least the wood cutting could be done anytime.

JW was getting accustomed to the daily work of the miner. His muscles no longer felt rubbery, nor were they as sore as they'd been the first few nights. Not every shift was as physically demanding as those had been. Sometimes, he and Mickey had to wait until the blasting was complete. JW was glad he didn't have to handle the blasting powder yet. He didn't mind drilling the holes, but the black powder was a volatile, unstable substance, and he was in no hurry to learn how to use it. He knew he might have to, but he preferred to load the coal. Mickey had told him that men had been seriously injured in explosions. Some had lost hands and some had been killed. The fuses sometimes didn't work properly, and when the miner tried to set another charge, often the original charge would go off, injuring him – or worse.

So many thoughts ran through his mind on the walk home. He was glad his father was almost better and that he could return to work soon. With everyone helping, the cow was getting milked and the animals fed.

JW's thoughts turned to Beth. He hoped the training and work wasn't too hard. Having to care for sick people was not something JW believed he could do. It was difficult enough seeing his father ill. To have to do it day in and day out seemed as mind-numbing as sitting in the dark opening a trap door. *Guess a lot of jobs aren't great*, he thought.

The wind had picked up a little, and there was a hint of the ocean in it. He could taste and smell the salt air and smiled at the thought of summers spent casting about on the lake with the raft's sail catching a gust of wind and rushing them twenty or so feet forward at a time. *A job on the ocean would be great*, JW thought. Yep, it sure would. He planned to talk to Alfred this evening about putting aside some hours to start learning how to build the boat.

As he came close to the house JW saw his parents and several people standing by the barn. Even Gulliver was there, paying no attention as he drew nearer.

"What's going on?" JW asked, and then noticed the potatoes and turnips piled in baskets.

"Alfred's family came to help out and harvested all the remaining crops," JW's mother said.

The four men who'd come with Alfred looked his way and nodded. They said their goodbyes to Alfred and headed toward the trees that lined the Donaldson's farm. They carried some of the vegetables with them, and JW saw that they had brought some of their own goods that they'd left with his mother.

"They did all this work and left fish and meat," Mary said.

JW saw the appreciation in his mother's eyes. He felt more than a little overwhelmed himself. He simply had to put the vegetables in the root cellar and his job was done.

"Wow," JW said. "Thank you, Alfred. And thank you," JW called, turning to look where the men had gone. They were standing at the edge of the woods and returned his wave.

"This will give you time to do other things than work. They are good men, and this is their way of saying thank you for the kindness you and your parents have shown me," Alfred said, as if answering the questions JW wanted to ask.

"Your father said you were swinging the hammer last evening, learning how to make tools. Shaping metal and working with wood have similarities. Both teach you to be patient."

JW was anxious to get started learning the new skills, but he knew that it was going to be a long, slow process and that he couldn't hurry the end result. "Well, you're the teacher, and I plan to pay close attention, but right now I am ready to eat." He quickly realized that everyone had been working outside all day, and supper might not be ready. "I can cook up some eggs if you didn't get supper ready," JW said.

"There's stew on the back of the stove and some biscuits and corn bread too. We all ate just before you got here. I got supper ready a little early to feed our guests – Alfred's family –before they left."

JW saw a streak of dirt across his father's forehead and knew that he had done some of the work too. He was thankful that he didn't look any worse for doing it. "Please excuse me while I have a quick bite, then I'll get busy putting all this away," JW said, waving his arm over the baskets and bags of vegetables in front of the barn doors. He was so happy. The men had saved him days of work and perhaps had saved much of the crop from being ruined by frost.

—

JW knocked on the shed door. He heard Alfred moving about inside.

"Come in."

"Hi, Alfred. I just wanted to thank you again for asking your family to complete the harvest."

"They are very kind men, willing to help when help is needed."

"Do they live close by?" JW asked.

"Yes, some do, in Little Bras d'Or. They fish and trap, and others work with their hands in wood. The traditional ways are very important to them, and they are very proud men and women. Some of the others continue to migrate to other parts of their lands, going where the spirit takes them."

"Do they have a lot of land?" JW asked.

Alfred clenched his jaw before he spoke. "All of what is known as Cape Breton, mainland Nova Scotia, Prince Edward Island and New Brunswick were Mi'kmaq lands," Alfred said. "The Europeans were granted fishing and trapping rights, but that was not enough for them. They wanted to own the land too, even if it wasn't included in their treaties. The Mi'kmaq lands diminished in size until all that is left today are small tracts the government chose for us — them.

"I'm sure if you asked your friend Smitty, he'd be able to tell about the mistreatment of his people by the Europeans and Americans. People were stolen from their lands and used as slaves to make the landowners rich. They fought hard to regain their freedom."

Almost as an afterthought, Alfred said in a low voice, "Freedom isn't free."

JW looked at his friend, at a loss for words.

"Perhaps it's the same the world over. Those with money and power don't want to share," Alfred said.

JW listened as Alfred gave him a history lesson that was not in any of the books he'd studied in school. He thought it was similar to what JB McLachlan said. Those in power lord it over others and take, and take, and take – without giving.

—

"Hiya, Patty. Who's your friend?"

"This here's, Donnie, Red. Glad to see ya back. I heard you were coming."

"Hi there, Donnie. I'm just covering the odd shift until Andy's back. I hear he's getting better. I also hear JW and Mickey are in tunnel twelve?"

"Yeah, I think Mickey wanted to go, but it was Anderson who told JW he was going too. They seem to be doing good, Red. I was talking to them," Patty said. "I spent a couple days there, but me and Donnie are gonna stay on the trap doors up here."

"I can't imagine Andy's too happy with JW down there. I gotta say, I prefer the rake to the cage myself," Red said. "Dropping like a rock off a cliff – well, it's not for me."

Patty realized that when someone like Red, who'd spent his life underground, admitted he didn't like the cage, it must truly be dangerous. He knew slope mining also had dangers; when the cable broke on the rake men could die too – and had – but there was something about the cage and shaft mining that was enough to make grown men afraid.

"Yep, that's why me and Donnie are staying up here. Glad to see ya back, Red," Patty said again.

"You boys have a good shift and try to stay awake," Red said.

"Oh we will, Red," Patty said, and Donnie nodded his assent.

Red smiled as he left the boys. He heard Patty talking to Donnie.

"Best bosses they ever had down here, him and Andy. On my first night, me and JW had a bit of a set-to, and Red let us off with a stern warning. Somebody like Anderson would have fired me before I got to work my first shift."

The voices of the boys carried a little ways; Red smiled and hoped they'd be safe. He was very happy to be no longer working every day. Fishing, hunting and tending his small garden filled his days nicely. His needs were simple, and fresh air was a wonderful thing. Red coughed and spat coal dust on the floor, as he had all those years he toiled underground, first as a miner and then as an overman. His bandy legs were no longer suited for walking the tunnels. Andy couldn't return quickly enough for him.

Chapter 25

"Hello, Beth. Hi, Sally," Davey Brown said, ignoring JW and Mickey. The four of them had been at the matinee and were now on Main Street. "I just got back from Cambridge," Davey said, continuing to speak only to the two girls. "Oh, I could have gone to Oxford, but my father is a Cambridge man, so I wanted to follow in his footsteps. Not, of course, in mining. Heavens no, there are too many troubles dealing with the lowly, uneducated hooligans – always wanting more. No I plan to travel and—"

"Yes, well we're in a hurry," Beth said. "Enjoy London," she added.

Beth held JW's hand tightly, feeling the tension in his arm. She turned and headed toward the centre of town. Mickey and Sally were talking about the film they'd just seen, and Beth and JW joined in.

"I don't think it is very polite to walk away in the middle of a conversation," Davey said, putting his hand on Beth's shoulder to stop her.

JW slapped Davey's hand away. "We don't have time to waste talking to you, Davey. Why not go and visit your friends?"

"I'm sure Beth can speak for herself."

Beth looked from JW to Davey. "As JW said, why not go and visit some friends? You've chosen not to be ours."

Davey looked at the four people in front of him but only took in Beth's face. He liked her and wanted a chance to show her. He blurted, "How can you choose a lowly paid coal miner over me?"

JW stood in front of Beth. "Davey, you've been asked nicely to go away."

The sudden punch to his face drove JW's head back, and he felt a trickle of blood in his mouth. He spat it at the feet of Davey, who now had his hands raised, his feet shifting side to side. A second punch glanced off JW's head. He quickly pulled his coat off and threw it to Mickey who stood watching what was not yet a fight, but soon would be.

Davey looked at JW. "My father is your boss and your sickly father's boss and probably that fellow's there with you."

JW blocked the next two punches and noticed a look of fear on Davey's face; clearly he was no longer as sure of the outcome as he'd been when he'd thrown the first couple of surprise blows. JW also noticed that Davey dropped his left as he moved forward, circling. A small crowd had gathered, and JW heard encouragement from some of the onlookers. He knew this wouldn't end well – regardless of the outcome.

In a low voice, JW said, "If you just want to end this now, we can," and saw a triumphant look on Davey's face. Clearly, he mistook the offer as fear. Davey sprang forward, dropping his left as he prepared to swing. The crushing blow from JW knocked him to the ground, where he lay unable to get back up.

After giving JW his coat, Mickey looked down at Davey who still hadn't made the move to get up. "Enjoy your travels, whoever you are, but leave the fighting to real men." Several in the crowd laughed.

JW cringed at Mickey's words. He wished Davey had stayed his friend instead of trying to steal Beth away from him. JW walked back to where Davey lay on the sidewalk.

The small crowd had dispersed, leaving Davey alone. Davey took JW's proffered hand and stood up. No words were exchanged, and JW caught up with the others.

"I woulda left him there, if it was me," Mickey said. "Especially since he came looking for it."

Beth looked at Mickey and JW. She liked Mickey but knew JW had a kinder heart. She understood living with Shawn McGuire and his bullying ways would have a negative influence on just about anyone, but was glad JW stood for what he believed was right. She hoped Mickey would come to learn the difference between winning and winning well.

"Nah, Mick, he just wants what he can't have, and it must be more than he can take. I wouldn't change places with him for all the money in the world," JW said, and squeezed Beth's hand. She squeezed back. He didn't know what would come of the altercation between him and Davey, but there was nothing he could do about it. If he did lose his job, it was way too late to get back to school. He pushed the thought away. He wanted to enjoy the rest of the day with Beth. They seldom had time off together.

"Yeah, I guess you're right," Mickey said. Laughing, he added, "Still, I wouldn't mind a little of his money."

JW laughed, and the girls joined in. They crossed the street and went into the Co-operative store. The selections seemed to be greater than usual, and JW realized that Christmas was less than two months away – time to start thinking about what to get Beth and his mother. He glanced at the bins and shelves spread throughout the store, filled with clothes, food and school supplies. A memory came flooding in, and he recalled his mother and his teacher, Mrs.

Johnson, talking three years earlier. Mrs. Johnson had all but pleaded for there to be some way for JW to attend high school, and his mother, who'd felt badly enough, had said there was no other way, that they'd fallen on hard times and JW had to go to work in the mines. Fortunately, his parents had found a way, and he was able to get three more years of schooling in before ending up where he'd never wanted to.

The bell above the Co-op's door clanged as shoppers entered, bringing JW's thoughts back to the present. The day was drawing to a close, and long shadows were cast on the street.

"I guess it's getting close to suppertime," JW said. "Don't want to be late for that," he said, smirking, and waited for Mickey's inevitable comment on his appetite.

"I wouldn't want to feed you," Mickey said. "It'd take all my pay to keep you full." They all laughed, knowing it was probably true.

They parted in front of the store. Sally and Mickey were going to his place for supper. "Da's off hunting and won't be back until tomorrow," Mickey explained. He'd told JW he didn't much like taking Sally there when his father was home.

There was crispness in the air as Beth and JW walked toward his house. Beth wanted to drop by and see Beauty. Although she'd like a cat of her own, she was content to visit Beauty. Now with her nursing studies, she wouldn't have time for a kitten, so this worked quite well. JW had been surprised the first time Beth had held Tennyson. The rat had squirmed for a second or two before sitting comfortably in her hand. Beth was careful to spend time with Tennyson if he was there when she visited.

"I'm sorry for what happened today," JW said.

"Me too," Beth said.

"You didn't do anything wrong."

"Neither did you. I thought Davey knew—"

"Oh, he knows, but – well I can't blame him for trying. I wish he hadn't started a fight though. Guess maybe he thought he'd impress you with Cambridge and his future plans to travel."

Beth put her arm around JW's waist and moved in closer to him as they continued toward the Donaldsons' farm. "Sally said Mickey is talking marriage," Beth said.

"We've been talking marriage. I mean when we're older, so I guess it's pretty normal," JW said.

"Sally said he was talking about getting married soon. Like really soon."

"What did Sally say?"

"She seemed to get flustered after telling me, and then one of the Sisters came in the lunch room. She never did tell me what she said. Hopefully they'll wait until after she finishes nursing training."

"Do you want to get married ... soon?" JW asked, his heart pounding, not sure of the answer he wanted to hear.

"I want to get married, but I'm not in a hurry, are you?"

"No, I'm in no hurry, but someday – for sure."

Beth stopped walking and took his hands in hers. Looking in his eyes, she stood on her tiptoes, and JW bent to kiss her, picking her off her feet with the hug that followed. Back on her feet, Beth said, "I imagine we'll have to figure out where we'll live and get all the stuff bought before we set up house."

"I never thought about all that, but yeah, I guess we'll have to save a lot of money to get our own place. I'm sure Ma and Da will give me ... us a piece of land, if you don't mind living there."

"Long as we have a roof over our heads, it doesn't matter where."

They walked and talked about JW's job and Beth's training until the house came into view.

"Is your hand sore, JW?"

"No."

"I'll bet his face is," Beth said, and they walked into the house.

Chapter 26

JW pulled a small brass plate from the hook and passed it to the man in the lamp house. The number on it corresponded with the one on his headlamp battery. The battery-operated headlamp replaced the old open flame type JW had used the first time he'd worked underground. He watched as the man placed his number on the board behind him. JW tried not to think about the purpose of the number but knew it was so that he could be identified if a cave-in happened. He changed into his work clothes and hung the others in their place. Thinking Mickey should be along soon, he stayed in the work area. He nodded to and talked with some of the men. Patty and Donnie were walking by on their way to the tunnel where he wished he was still working, rather than in tunnel twelve. He waved and got two in return.

"JW, I need a word."

JW turned to the voice, worried about what was to come. "Yes sir, Mr. Brown." He followed him into the office. Dayshift seemed to have a lot more office staff around than backshift.

Without any other greeting, Mr. Brown began. "David came home the other day, and all I got from him is that you struck him. Is this true?"

JW heard the tension in Davey's father's voice and thought it likely he would be returning home instead of going to work. Although JW didn't think it right for Mr. Brown to use his position as mine manager to settle his son's affairs, that was what was happening. "Yes, sir, it's true." JW prepared himself to hear he'd lost his job and wondered if his actions were going to affect his father's work too.

"Would you care to explain this for me?"

JW, surprised by the request, took a few moments to collect his thoughts. After he related what had caused the fight and that he hadn't thrown the first punch, Mr. Brown nodded.

"You best get ready. Your shift will be starting soon."

"Yes, sir," JW said, and left the office. He hoped that would be the last of it. He put on his helmet, attached the battery to his belt and got ready for his shift.

—

"I think I'll take a walk to town," Andrew said. He smiled at Mary. "It'll feel good being back at work. Not so much the underground part, but the routine ... and the money."

"Seeing you healthy is the most important part," Mary said. In the past month her husband had gained back all of his weight and perhaps a few more pounds as well. He'd seemed to enjoy his time working with JW and Alfred. "And if I need a new poker or coal shovel, I know someone who can make them," she added.

"I forgot how much I enjoyed making things. Might be a sideline if things ... when things drop off at the mines. JW picked it up quite quickly, so I might get him to make the tools you need."

"Oh I think he's got lots to keep him busy, with Beth and then with Alfred's lessons. You'll be starting on dayshift?"

"Yes. I wanted to go to tunnel twelve with JW and Mickey, but Mr. Brown told me to start back in the other tunnel to replace Anderson. At least I'll get to keep an eye on the younger boys. I imagine Red'll be glad I'm coming back too. But I'll occasionally go down tunnel twelve to check on the boys," Andrew said, and saw a look of relief on Mary's face.

"How was he?"

"Red? I'm not—"

"No, Mr. Brown."

"Seemed okay. Like most fathers, I'm sure he just wants to look out for his son. I wish it hadn't happened, but I would do the same if someone laid a hand on you. Just glad me and JW still have jobs. I'll be home in time for supper."

"You better be, because now that you're all mended, JW won't leave you any." They both laughed as Andrew left the house to head for town.

As he walked along Main Street, Andrew waved to Long Jack in the streetcar. The noise coming from inside the tavern made him stop. He looked through the doors and saw there was a large crowd of men drinking away some of their meagre pay. Unfortunately, he knew, there were a few that would spend more than they could afford.

The thought of a cold beer appealed to him, and he went inside. Almost immediately, he wished he hadn't, because some of the noise was being produced by Shawn McGuire, whose temperament got worse when he drank. The man sitting next to Shawn, Andrew quickly realized, was Anderson, who seemed quite comfortable accepting the beer that Shawn was buying for him.

JW had told Andrew that when Anderson sent him to tunnel twelve, it had seemed like a punishment.

"Anderson, Shawn. Good news, Anderson, I'm back to work on Monday, and you get to go back to the other side." A few of the men close by clapped Andrew on the back, and one of them said, "Glad you're coming back, Andy boy."

"It'll be me and you again, Shawn." The sheepish look on McGuire's face meant he got the message.

"That's good, then, Donaldson. I'll be glad to get back," Anderson said, louder than needed.

Moving closer to Anderson, Andrew spoke in a quiet voice, "If I find out that you sent my boy below as a favour to McGuire, I'll be paying you a visit."

Anderson stared into Andrew's eyes for a moment before looking away. He got up and left the tavern.

—

Davey pushed open the door and looked at the high ceilings in the house he'd lived in for almost five years. Although there were two fires burning throughout the day, the house always seemed cold. He guessed for some, being an only child would bring special treatment. But he and his father had never developed a bond. As he started up the stairs to his bedroom, Davey noticed the door to his father's study was open. Usually the door was closed. He saw his father look up and then beckon him to come in.

"I spoke to JW Donaldson today."

Davey feared what was coming next.

"He told me you threw the first punch, actually several. Is this true?"

Davey nodded, not trusting his voice.

"Well, what do you have to say for yourself?"

Davey stared at his father for a moment before averting his gaze, dropping his eyes to his father's desk, waiting to be dismissed.

Mr. Brown sat down and picked up a piece of correspondence, signalling the meeting was over. Davey turned and left the room. When he reached the stairs, he heard his father call out.

"I'll bet you told that boy you were at Cambridge. Did you happen to mention it was in Massachusetts, not London? And that you're in boarding school, not university?"

Davey treated them as rhetorical questions. He didn't plan to answer, nor did his father expect him to. Davey knew the fact that his mother had to collect him from boarding school because he was so homesick was an embarrassment to his father. Although his father hadn't yet mentioned the lost tuition for the missed semester, he would.

Chapter 27

The light dusting of snow made the fields look like a Christmas picture JW had seen at the Co-op. Except for a few of Gulliver's paw prints, the snow cover was pristine. JW was excited to have the next couple of days off. He planned to spend them working on the boat with Alfred during the day and walking to meet Beth in the late afternoon.

With his father recovered and back at work, JW had more time to spend doing other things than chores. It had taken quite a while to locate the cedar, pine and other trees that were to be used in the boat's construction. The small sawmill in town had agreed to cut the planking JW would need, and he'd agreed to work off what he owed or provide additional wood for the owner. Today was the day the lumber was to be delivered.

Alfred had made the plans for the boat so it would fit perfectly through the barn door once it was finished. He had taught JW how to make tree nails, the wooden dowels that would be used to hold the planks in place, along with the iron nails his father had made in the forge. He had also been instructing JW in the steaming method used to bend the wood. JW hadn't imagined that a piece of wood could be bent into such strange shapes until Alfred had shown him. JW was pleased with the decision to use the caravel design instead of the clinker design. The hull was smoother where the planks butted together instead of overlapping. It sounded like more work, but it would give the hull a more streamlined look.

Although they were building a boat, Alfred was also instructing JW how to build a ship. Learning what all the different parts of the ship were called was an eye-opener. JW had known fore and aft and starboard and port and some other terms, but he'd had no idea that the frame of the ship consisted of ribs, nor what various thwarts were or what a quarter knee was. Alfred showed him those and many other parts, and JW spent time studying them – he didn't mind when Alfred corrected him when he made a mistake.

With so much preparatory work required, JW was happy when Mickey and Smitty had shown up on some of their days off. Smitty knew what he was doing, and Mickey was willing to learn. With their help, the boat's cradle was now built.

Smitty was very interested in the shipbuilding process and seemed to know much of what Alfred taught. Smitty explained that it had been quite a number of years since he'd been on or near a ship – not since leaving Barbados. Alfred surprised JW when he told Smitty that he had spent time there as a young man, and JW listened enviously as they talked of the white sandy beaches. He saw the longing in Smitty's eyes as they spoke of his beloved homeland.

"Looks like you and Smitty might have to draw straws for the first mate's job," JW had said one day.

Having learned that the first mate was usually required to keep a log, Mickey replied, "As long as I'm part of the crew, Smitty can be first mate."

JW smiled at the recollection, thinking that if it was a full-sized ship, large enough to sail an ocean, Smitty would definitely be the best choice for first mate. He couldn't imagine Mickey wanting to learn what everything was called, much less plot a course.

—

When he entered the barn, JW wasn't surprised to see Alfred already laying out the tools needed for the day. JW found the tools were becoming more recognizable. He had watched his father make some of them and had helped with making a few himself.

Alfred was humming a tune as he laid out some milk for Beauty and walked a few steps to drop some oats for Tennyson. JW thought it quite funny that Tennyson sometimes waited for his meal of oats to be laid out for him rather than going into Lightning's stall where he could have eaten all he wanted any day. *Perhaps he just likes the company*, JW thought.

JW heard something and went to the door to look up the road. "Here comes the lumber now," he said.

He grinned as the horse and wagon pulled up to the barn and was still grinning as he watched them head back toward town a short time later. He could hardly wait to get started with the building. He knew it would take many months to get the boat built, especially with the limited time he had after work, but even if they could get the frame started, he would be happy.

"It's good the wood has arrived," Alfred said.

JW nodded. "This is great."

Once they had loaded all the planks in the barn, it was time for lunch. All that lumber, lying neatly in piles, made JW anxious to eat and get back out to the barn.

Chapter 28

JW stood at the back of the cage, Mickey next to him. The large metal roof jacks and several coils of rope took up most of the remaining space. Four other men were squeezed in. There was a squeaking sound as the cage adjusted to the additional weight.

"Hope the cable holds," one of the men said.

"Not funny, Gerry," another man said.

As the single bar was being lowered across the opening, JW's father stepped in and pulled the bar in place. The descent began immediately. JW was surprised to see his father; he wasn't working tunnel twelve. And JW knew his father wouldn't have gotten on the cage had he known his son was on it too. There was an unwritten rule that two members of the same family never travelled together in the same cage – a superstitious belief that doing so was asking for trouble. He was about to call out to his father when the normal squeaking sound turned into groaning, then suddenly the cage was free-falling. The cable had snapped.

The men braced themselves for the crash that would come as they hit the floor hundreds of feet below. They knew they were going to die. Eyes wide open, resignation on their faces, no one said anything, but some lips moved in silent prayer. JW thought of his mother losing him and his father, and then he thought of Beth. Mickey stood beside him with his eyes closed to tiny slits, teeth gritted together.

As the cage hurtled downward, JW's father looked toward him and JW saw the shock of recognition on his face. Andrew tried to squeeze toward the back, closer to him. The cage seemed to pick up speed, then began scraping against one side of the shaft then the other, digging deep gashes into the wall. Suddenly, the weight of the roof jacks shifted. The cage started to slow down, then came to an abrupt halt, throwing the men to the floor of the cage. The cage was wedged in the shaft at a forty-five degree angle. JW watched in horror as the jacks slid sideways, toppled over and crushed two men. One of them was Gerry, the man who had joked about the cable holding.

JW slowly pulled himself to his knees. He felt blood running down his face, some finding its way into his left eye. He tried to wipe the blood away, but he couldn't lift his arm. He had been holding onto the side of the cage when it hit the wall of the shaft.

JW squinted his good eye and saw light below. It looked like they were only about six or seven feet from the bottom.

"Are you alright, JW?" his father asked.

"Just banged up some, Da, but I think I'm okay."

Mickey wasn't moving, but JW heard him moan and hoped he'd be okay. The other men at the back of the cage were slowly starting to get to their feet. Then Mickey came around and, although still groggy, managed to get up onto his hands and knees. "Mickey's up and around too, Da."

JW saw his father move toward the men trapped by the metal jacks.

"Dear, God," Andrew whispered. "Gerry and Artie, they're both gone. Two real good men."

JW noticed that his father was holding his side and hoped he'd only bruised his ribs. Andrew sprang into action, first ensuring that no one needed immediate medical attention. One of the other two men called out, "We're okay, Andy. We just gotta get outta here, is all."

"Working on it," was his father's reply. "Looks like there's enough room for us to fit between the cage and the wall." He grabbed one of the coils of rope lying on the floor of the cage. JW watched him secure a bowline knot to one of the jacks that had slid against the side of the cage. He knew the knot used to tow boats would hold and wouldn't slip as the men lowered themselves to the floor below. JW figured he would have to go last as he had little use of his left arm.

There were shouts from below. Andrew called to them, "We're coming down." The men near the door went first, followed by Mickey.

"You go next," his father said.

"Can't use my left arm," JW said, and grimaced as he tried to move it. "You go first, then you can grab my legs to ease me down."

"Do you think it's broke?" Andy asked.

"Don't know if it's my arm or my shoulder, but it's not working right. How we gettin' outta here?" JW asked, and rubbed his eye, trying to clear his vision. The bleeding from his head had slowed.

"Maintenance crew will hook up a new cable to the cage, and once they get it unwedged from the wall of the shaft, it'll be back in business."

JW and his father glanced at where Gerry and Artie lay. Then Andrew moved into place, grunting as his side pressed against the metal frame of the cage. A few seconds later, he was down and called for JW to follow.

JW knelt on the floor then lay on his belly before taking the rope in his one useable hand. He backed toward the edge of the cage floor, his shoulder screaming in pain. He held tightly as he let his legs dangle over the edge, then he was in space with no way to get back up. Without help, he would crash to the floor below. Panic started to overwhelm him until he felt strong arms grab his legs.

Safe on the floor of the mine, JW moved to where Mickey and the other men were sitting. Mickey said he was fine, but there was a large lump on his head, and he had a nasty gash there too. Everyone had cuts that would need tending. JW realized how lucky they were. Gerry and Artie would never go home again.

It was hours before the cage was once again able to be used. JW and Mickey looked at each other as they were helped to the cage. It had been pulled to the surface, and the jacks and dead men had been removed, but there was blood everywhere.

JW's father moved to get on the cage, but one of the men said, "I ain't getting on if the two of you are gonna be on it at the same time. Already caused one accident," he said.

"Yeah, you four go up in this one," Andy said. He hoped the men weren't going to blame him for the accident, but he knew it would at least be spoken behind his back, perhaps for a long time. "Tell them to send it right back. I'll see ya topside in a few minutes, JW."

"Okay, Da," JW said, and watched as the bar was pulled into place. He held his breath as the ride to the surface started, and he released it only as the cage jolted to a stop. Stepping out, he heard Mickey tell someone that there was one more injured man to come up.

JW saw managers and other men from the office scurrying about. One of them barked, "Clean up the mess and get back to work. We've got orders to fill."

Orders to fill, thought JW. No mention of the injured men or the loss of life and what that was going to mean to the families left behind. JW caught the eye of Mr. Brown, and they looked at each other for a time. Then Mr. Brown turned away without even a nod or a hint of sadness. JW felt anger rising within him. What he'd heard JB McLachlan say about "us and them" was actually true. *Until we face that it's us and them, or us against them and all their dirty tactics, we'll never get what we want or need.*

JW remembered again how Red, the man his father replaced as overman, told him years ago that the owners cared more about the horses than the men, because horses cost money and men didn't, men were free.

JW felt his pulse quicken. He wasn't sure whether it was from the realization he'd come so close to death or because it mattered little to the mine owners and managers.

Chapter 29

Beth listened to the Sister as she informed them that there'd been an accident in the mine and injured men could be arriving soon. Beth glanced to where Sally sat, and their eyes met. So far, they had been caring mostly for the elderly. They were told to be ready for possibly severe injuries. Beth had thought they would have spent more time studying, but one of the nuns had told her "hands-on experience is the best teacher."

After stocking the shelves with bandages and supplies, there was little to do but wait. When the bodies of Gerry and Artie arrived, Beth and Sally were shocked. Sally's crying startled the nuns, whose stern looks did nothing to stifle her sobs. But Beth quickly explained that Artie was Sally's uncle, her mother's brother. Sally was quietly ushered from the room by one of the younger nuns. Beth passed the nuns' visual inspection – they could see she wasn't about to faint – and although she was saddened by the deaths of the two men, she knew she had a job to do. She tried to hide the tremors in her hands.

The strong antiseptic smell struck JW as he and Mickey entered Hamilton Memorial Hospital. His father drew a pain-filled breath when he opened the door for them, one hand going to his side. As JW shuffled forward, his right hand holding his left arm tightly against his stomach, he noticed a gurney pushed against a wall with a sheet pulled over the body resting on it. He wondered if it was Gerry or Artie.

As if sensing his thoughts, Andrew placed a hand on his son's shoulder. "Tough, tough day. We're lucky to be alive."

"I know we're lucky, Da. Poor Artie and Gerry," JW said. Mickey had slowed his walk and nodded his head. JW added, "I don't even know the other two who were on the cage with us."

"They're good men—"

"Come in, Mr. Donaldson," the nurse said, interrupting him. "We have to take a look at that arm of yours."

JW realized she was speaking to him and smiled, despite the trauma of the day. Mr. Donaldson was a salutation he thought better suited his father.

"Thank you, Sister." He entered the examination room, the nurse following behind. He was surprised to see Beth in the room and saw her eyes widen in recognition. She hadn't seen him in full miners' dress before. His hands and face were darkened a little, but nothing like they were after a full shift underground.

"What happened?" the nurse asked.

"The cable on the cage broke. Gerry and Artie were killed and five of us got off lucky," JW said. He wasn't sure if they needed more information, so he waited to be asked.

"You were on the same cage as the men killed?" Beth blurted out, fear in her voice.

"Yes, me and Mickey, and Da and two more men."

As the nurse began to clean the cut on JW's head, she looked at Beth. "You know each other?"

Beth blushed. "He's my boyfriend. We finished grade eleven together, then JW went to the mine to help out his family. He was the smartest boy in the school," she gushed.

The sister nodded. "We'll X-ray your left arm, but I think you're also going to need some stitches on that head, to keep all those brains in."

JW and Beth laughed, and a little tension left the room. JW drew a sudden breath as the nurse moved his arm to remove his jacket in preparation for the X-ray.

"Oh dear, at least two of your fingers look swollen, so we better make sure they are X-rayed too," the nun said.

JW looked at his hand and tried moving his fingers, but his shoulder pain overrode any other pain he might have felt. He heard the nurse tell Beth that his shoulder looked dislocated or broken, perhaps both.

They helped JW into a wheelchair, and Beth pushed it down the hallway to where the X-ray machine was located.

"Da seems to have hurt his ribs, so he'll probably need an X-ray too," JW told her. "Maybe Mickey and the other men as well. Mickey was knocked out." He caught a glimpse of his father and Mickey and one of the other men. "Where's the other man, Beth?" JW said in a low voice, trying to look over his shoulder at Beth.

"There's just the four of you that came in. Maybe the other felt well enough to go home."

"I think everyone was battered and bruised. We're just lucky—"

"Bring him right in. We're ready to go," the doctor said.

"Yes, doctor. Sister said to mention his fingers on his left hand as well," Beth said, as she pushed JW into the room.

"Let's have a look."

Beth smiled at JW and turned to leave.

"I may need some help. It looks as if the shoulder is dislocated, and if it is, I'll need you to hold him steady as I pull it back into place."

"Yes, doctor," Beth answered.

JW felt a rush of anxiety as he thought of the pain already throbbing in his shoulder. He could only imagine the pain it would cause if the doctor pulled on it. Crying out in front of Beth would be embarrassing. The doctor told him to let go of his arm so it could be X-rayed. Next came his fingers. He gritted his teeth to endure the pain. Once the X-rays were taken, JW and Beth sat in the hallway, waiting for them to be developed. She held his right hand in hers, and they spoke quietly, trying to come to terms with what had happened.

"The good news, your arm is not broken; however, the shoulder is dislocated. Two of your fingers are broken. We'll get the shoulder done first, then splint the fingers."

The news didn't seem particularly good to JW, but apparently it was better than the shoulder being broken. JW sat on the gurney and felt his muscles tighten as the doctor gripped his left arm.

"Beth, hold him still as I rotate the arm to get the shoulder back into place."

Beth linked her hands together under his left arm, and JW felt her warm breath against his neck. Through gritted teeth, he drew a deep breath as the doctor moved his arm out from his body. Suddenly, JW felt his shoulder pop back into place, and there was an immediate relief from the pain he'd been suffering. He closed his hands into fists and quickly became aware of the pain in his fingers. Moments later, splints were on his fingers and several stitches closed his cut. He sat still as Beth put the bandage on, impressed by her skill. They walked together back to where JW's father sat. Beth squeezed JW's arm as they parted.

"Thanks, Nurse Beth," JW said.

"Oh, you're welcome, sir," she said to JW, and she smiled at his father.

"Mickey's in being seen, and I should be next," Andrew told his son. "You look a tad more comfortable than earlier."

"Yeah, the shoulder was dislocated, not broken. Just have to wear it in this sling for a while. Might be two or three weeks before I can get back to work."

"By the looks of that hand, it will longer than that before you'll be loading any coal. Besides, your mother will have something to say about you and working in the mines."

"It's not like I have a lot of choice. I have to work, and it's pretty much the only thing around. If we lived in Sydney, I might be able to get on at the steel plant."

"There's injury and death there too, JW. I don't know of many jobs that are a hundred percent safe."

JW sat beside his father, waiting until Mickey came out and his father went in. Mickey's mother had also been waiting, and JW saw the sad look on her face as she put her arms around her son. JW was sure she didn't want Mickey to be in the mines, but it was the only way of life she knew. Her father had worked there, as well as her husband, and now her son did too. JW knew they needed the money Mickey brought in to help feed his brother and sisters. JW's thoughts went to Gerry's and Artie's families. A lot had happened today.

He remembered what the mine manager had said: "Clean up the mess and get back to work. We've got orders to fill." No mention of the dead men. *Us and them.* The thought kept coming into JW's mind, but he didn't want to believe it. He didn't want to believe that money was more important than the men sent underground. His thoughts were interrupted when his father came out of the examination room.

"Nothing broken, just badly bruised. A day or two, and I'll be good to go," Andrew said.

"That's good then. I imagine the ribs'll be sore for a while though."

"I might be walking a little slower for a few days, but at least I don't have to shovel coal," Andrew said, and smiled. "Guess we better get home. Your Ma'll be worried sick about us. I'm sure she's heard the news by now."

The sun was bright as they walked through the hospital's doors. JW looked out over Sydney Harbour. The water was a little rough; small whitecaps danced on the surface. A freighter carrying iron ore was on its way to the steel plant, its stacks billowing black smoke into the air.

"There's your mother, and Alfred," his father said. They were coming down the path in the cart behind Lightning.

JW was happy to see them and glad that Lightning was there to take them home. The walk home was tiring most times, but it would have been much worse today.

On the trip home, Mary sat between her husband and her son, her head swivelling between them as she asked what had happened. Alfred sat quietly holding the reins, listening but not saying anything. JW saw the expression on Alfred's face change as he listened to the part about the cable breaking and the cage finally coming to a stop six feet from the floor below. There was a sudden silence. Everyone was exhausted, and there was nothing left to say. JW knew his mother would have lots more questions in the coming days, but for now they all sat quietly and listened to the wheels crunching against the road.

Chapter 30

"I wasn't expecting to see Uncle Artie – dead. I mean, it was a shock, Mickey," Sally said as Mickey hugged her to him. She started crying again.

"I know it must've been hard, but Beth said you're doin' real good at nursing. You should think about it some more before quittin'," Mickey said.

"You said a while back that we could get married, and I wouldn't have to think about nursing, 'cause the mining pay would do us. Besides, you don't know what it was like seeing Uncle Artie like that."

Mickey shook his head. He had heard her say that very thing several times and had nodded and hugged her, but he felt that something had to be said. "Yes I do, Sally. I was in the cage with 'em when they died, and if I hadda been a few feet closer, I mighta got crushed with them, instead of just this gash on my head. But I gotta go back to work in a couple of days in that same cage. I don't want to, but what can I do?"

Sally and Mickey stared into each other's eyes. They had spent the day with Beth and JW looking at the boat's progress and had stayed behind in the barn after JW left to walk Beth home. Sally petted Beauty but was a little nervous of Tennyson and let out a little gasp when Mickey reached down and picked him up. Tennyson sat on his arm, eating oats from his outstretched hand. Sally made Mickey wash his hands in the water bucket after he put him down. She petted the cow and Lightning but stopped short of trying to pet the chickens. Alfred was asleep on his cot in the shed.

"C'mon up in the hayloft," Mickey said. "There's a nice view of the water. See the window up there?"

"Yeah."

"C'mon then," Mickey said, pointing out the ladder. He went up first, then held his hand out to her.

Sally looked at the water and the trees off in the distance. She could just make out the eagle's nest next to where they'd gone swimming the past summer. "It is a beautiful view, Mickey," she said, moving closer to him. "It would be nice to have a place like this some day after we're married." She put her arms around Mickey, leaned into him and kissed him. She giggled as they lost their balance and tumbled into the soft hay. Neither hurried to get back up, and they continued to kiss.

Alfred woke from his nap, sat up and stretched from one side to the other, listening to his old joints crack. He was working a little harder than usual these days. He wanted JW to have his boat ready for the coming spring. Once he was sure JW understood how the pieces went together, Alfred helped to move things along to the next step. He was glad JW kept notes for future projects he might do on his own. He marvelled at how good a student he was. If JW wished to have a real ship one day, Alfred knew he could use a variation of this scaled-down version to build one. *This boat should bring him much pleasure on the lake*, he thought.

Alfred stoked the stove, and the fire came to life. He pulled the kettle over to the middle of the stove and walked out into the barn looking for Beauty. He saw her playing with a piece of twine hanging from a nail. It amazed him the simple things that brought her such joy. He smiled. He cocked his ear, thinking he'd heard a sound. Quickly, he located the source. Giggling, and it was coming from the hayloft.

Alfred coughed and watched two heads come into view. JW's friends, Sally and Mickey, quickly came down the ladder, blushing at getting caught in the hayloft. Alfred smiled at the two who stood there picking stalks of hay from each other's hair.

"I was just showing her the view from the window there," Mickey said, pointing to the loft, and Sally nodded.

"Yes, it's a pretty view from there," Alfred said. "I'm making some tea. Would you like a cup?"

"No thank you, sir. I should be getting home," Sally said.

"Thanks, Alfred, but we gotta go. See you soon. The ship— boat, is comin' along nice. Hope it'll be ready for the summer. See ya," Mickey said, and hurried behind Sally out the barn door and on their way toward town.

—

Following the accident there were two funerals in the town, attended by large crowds. Sitting with his parents, JW had glanced around the church and saw several of the managers from the mines. Mr. Brown was there, as well as the man who'd wanted the mess cleaned up. JW's eyes met JB McLachlan's several pews over. JB winked at him, and JW nodded. There was at least twice the usual Sunday crowd. JW understood that wakes and funerals were something of a social event. People got a chance to offer condolences and to catch up on any gossip while enjoying a first-rate lunch. JW was there out of respect for Gerry and Artie and their families, but he knew that some people showed up only for the sake of appearances.

It had been three days since the funerals, and JW had spent some time out in the barn with Alfred. Smitty had dropped by to help with the boat on his day off and, after spending the day working on the boat, had carried enough wood into the house to keep the stove going for a week or more. Although Smitty was more than ten years his senior, he and JW were friends, and JW realized that Smitty was the definition of a true friend, being there when needed, without being asked.

JW loved seeing the boat come together. He checked the plans on a regular basis. Geometry was important, and JW was glad he had paid attention in school. The frame was there now, each rib secured in place. There was a long way to go before it would be finished, but it seemed like a reality as he ran his hands over the different woods they had used, inhaling their various scents.

JW's father had started back to work on the dayshift today, and JW hoped he'd be okay. He was no longer making a face when he moved, so JW figured his ribs were healing and that he'd be fine, as long as he didn't overdo it. JW would likely be returning to work himself in another two to three weeks, now that his shoulder and fingers were feeling better. He was filled with a sudden rush of dread as he thought of stepping back into the cage the first time.

JW pushed down thoughts of the cage and decided now was the time to finally start reading the book he'd gotten months earlier, *The Bitter Cry of the Children*. Once he began reading it, he realized the title suited it well. The material was heart-rending. JW could hardly believe some of the accounts of what children had had to endure. He was horrified by the harrowing working conditions that children as young as four, five, six – mere babies – had suffered, all so that the wealthy owners could get richer.

Reading about how poverty and the lack of proper food for children would have lasting negative effects throughout their lifetime was eye-opening too. One section about a boy whose parents had signed papers saying he was older than his age struck a chord, and JW remembered his own parents had been forced by difficult times to do that very thing three years earlier, so that he could work as a trapper boy. Donnie's mother was forced to do the same.

As JW got further along in the book, he better understood JB McLachlan's indignation about working conditions. Without the men fighting for their rights, the owners of the mines, and any other businesses, would continue to treat workers as their property, with little or no regard for their well-being. JW realized too that the struggle couldn't be left only to the men.

He knew that he and Mickey, Patty and Donnie, and all the other boys had to become part of it. He understood that many people with power used it to keep others down. He saw it in the way some miners mistreated the trapper boys, making an already miserable job even worse. Although he and Mickey were no longer working the trap door, he felt it important to make sure all the people working underground were treated fairly.

JW felt sleep overtake him as he tried to read some more in bed that night. The book fell from his hands, hitting his chest, before dropping to the floor with a soft thud. The faces of Gerry and Artie filled his dreams as he slept fitfully.

Chapter 31

JW climbed the few steps to the front porch of the house and knocked on the door.

"Good afternoon, JW."

"Afternoon, Mrs. McLachlan. Is JB ... Mr. McLachlan home?"

"Who is it, Kate?" JW heard from inside.

"It's JW Donaldson. Go right in," Kate said, and smiled as he removed his shoes once he crossed the threshold.

"Bring him in, dear," JB said, a moment before JW entered the room.

"Afternoon, JB," JW said. They had dispensed with formalities years before.

"What brings you here, son?"

JW held out the book, *The Bitter Cry of the Children*. He waited while JB opened it and skimmed some of the pages. He watched JB nod his head in some places and grunt in others. JW said, "Much of what you've told me over the years is in this book. I thought maybe you were exaggerating, but I can see now you weren't."

"No, JW. And I was trying not to tell the worst of it. But man's quest for money puts it first, and all else second."

JW told JB what one of the mine managers had said just as he and Mickey and the other men arrived on the surface after the cage cable had broken. Barking orders about cleaning up the mess because there were orders to fill, with no regard for the dead or injured.

A look of rage crossed JB's face, quickly replaced with a forced calm expression. "I was going to rant and roar about the mistreatment, but I can see you've got a good grasp of what's going on," he said.

"Starting to, JB. I was thinking that things would just get better with time. I didn't realize all the hard work that was done to get the owners to part with a few more cents for the men. Now I know that unless you stand up and fight, things could get as bad or worse than when Roy the Wolf was running things."

"Yes, Roy Wolvin didn't care back when he was company president, and I'm not convinced these new guys do either. Have to keep on top of things all the time. The Union needs some young blood, like you. You should think about being more active in it."

"Maybe," JW said.

"The thing to know is that real change can be dangerous, because you have to challenge those in power."

JW realized that JB was probably referring to the time he'd spent in jail years earlier, which had cost him more than just time away from his family. JW's father had told him that the charges had been trumped up to get JB out of the way, to weaken the men's fight. His attempts to get elected to government had been, so far, unsuccessful. JW thought JB would make a good teacher, because he kept driving home a point until he was sure the person or people he was talking to understood.

JW wasn't entirely sure exactly why he'd come to visit JB. Maybe it was to tell him that, because of the book, he now believed much of what JB had told him over the years. Or maybe it was to listen to JB talk about us and them, a rallying cry to stand against the mine owners. But it was also to get JB's advice about something.

"JB, I've been thinking about how some of the men pick on the boys that have to work below. Shouldn't they treat them better?"

"In a perfect world, son. They should be kinder to them, but a mean man on the surface doesn't turn kinder by going into the mine. No, some of them get even meaner."

"Doesn't that make it harder to stand together when we're fighting for our rights?"

"I guess that's something we have to work on too."

—

JW sat in his room thinking about the hour he'd spent talking with JB. The stories the older man told of the previous generation's fight for rights made sense to him now, how the incremental steps forward were often followed by management pushing two or three steps backward. Profit above people was the owners' position, or at least it seemed that way to JW. The more he read the book about the plight of working children and their parents, the more he realized the owners wouldn't change unless they were forced to.

JW looked out the window at the barn and thought of the boat coming to life behind its walls. He just wanted to be a kid for a while longer, but his mind filled with thoughts of work, misery and money. The worries of the adult world seemed to be crashing in,

JW saw the need for the JB McLachlans of the world to move workers' rights forward, but he knew that sometimes the passionate message got lost and JB instead appeared pompous. JW believed that sometimes what was needed was a book like *The Bitter Cry of the Children* to state the facts and let the message pull at the heartstrings. The adults were so beaten down by the owners that they spent their time trying to get better pay for themselves. No one was left to speak for the children. JW hoped he could become a voice for his friends at least.

—

JW looked out over the water. Although the ocean was a mile off in the distance, he could see it clearly from the top of the Sydney Mines post office. He'd never dreamed he'd ever get to see the ocean from this vantage point. When he'd mentioned to Beth that he wished he could stand on the top of the building, she'd told him she would ask her uncle, who was the postmaster, if he'd be allowed. Months had passed since they'd spoken of it, and JW was surprised and excited to learn that his wish had been granted.

As a boy, he'd imagined the post office as a castle, centrally located, archers poised and ready to protect the town from foreign invaders. He still looked up at it in awe from street level, but being on the roof, seeing the town spread out before him, gave him a glimpse of what it must have been like for the kings and knights of old, gazing upon their lands.

From where he stood, the poverty of the community was no longer hidden but highlighted. He saw the houses lined in rows, smoke billowing from chimneys, heaps of coal ash and garbage piled high in the tiny backyards. He remembered when he'd studied Britain's Industrial Revolution and hand-drawn pictures detailing the poverty of those times. The similarity was chilling. He spotted Mickey's house and remembered the small garden Mickey's mother and sisters had planted in the little patch of dirt behind their house. The stunted harvest would have been laughable if it hadn't been so pitiful.

Pushing the sobering thoughts from his mind, he looked out again over the water, taking in the breathtaking view. A light breeze was blowing across the ocean's surface, causing a small spray of water to dance high into the air. Seagulls hovered, perhaps following a school of mackerel, hoping for smaller ones to come closer to the surface to provide an early morning meal. JW saw a few fishing boats, perhaps after those very mackerel or some cod. The official arrival of winter wasn't far off, and the dreaded ice and cold would soon force the fishermen to tie up their boats until spring.

JW hoped his boat would be ready come spring, or maybe summer. He thrilled at the idea of his lightweight boat skimming the surface of the ocean on a voyage to somewhere exciting but knew a voyage on the Bras d'Or Lake was the best he could hope for. He breathed deeply, inhaling the salt air that somehow carried inland to where he stood. Leaning forward, JW closed his hand over the brick wall and quickly realized that his fingers were not yet fully healed. His shoulder felt fine, but it would be another little while before he would be ready to load coal.

JW looked at Main Street below and saw Davey Brown carrying a small suitcase and walking toward the train station with his father. They stopped, and Davey and Mr. Brown shook hands. JW thought it an awkward exchange between father and son. He moved back from the wall, hoping he'd not been seen, as he didn't want to intrude on their parting. He assumed Davey was off to spend part of his Christmas break with other family before heading back to Cambridge.

A feeling of envy washed over JW when he thought of the opportunities available to Davey: the places he would visit and the things he'd get to see. But he quickly took stock and understood that Davey envied him a little, perhaps a whole lot, because of Beth. He moved closer to the edge and saw that Davey had continued on his own toward the train station. JW watched as he turned to where his father had been standing, to wave, but his father had already left, hurrying down the sidewalk. A new feeling washed over JW, one of sadness, as he watched Davey, shoulders slumped, turn back toward the train station.

—

It was mid-December, and the boat continued to take shape. JW and his parents convinced Alfred to move into the house for the nights. They were worried that he would be cold, as the temperature had dropped below freezing. Alfred had only protested slightly, claiming he didn't want to be a burden.

JW had gone to Beth's house for supper, because she had the day off.

"Show me your hand," Beth said.

JW held out his hand and tried not to wince as Beth moved his fingers back and forth. "See, all better," he said.

"Be sure they are, because I imagine once you go back to work, it will be hard on your fingers."

"Da said he's gonna start me out on a trap door for a week or so, so it should be no problem. And thank you, Nurse Beth."

Beth blushed. "You're welcome, Miner Boy. I wish you never had to go back in the mines."

"Me too, but there's not much else around. I'm as careful as can be, and hopefully the new cable means the cage will be safe for a long time."

"Have you seen Mickey this week?"

"No, he's back to work in tunnel twelve. But last week he told me that it was pretty scary when he had to step into the cage on his first shift back, and that he closed his eyes as the cage dropped."

Beth shuddered. "Sally said he's quieter since the accident. For a while, I thought she was going to quit the nursing program. I was worried the two of them would hurry up and get married. I'm glad she didn't quit."

"Yeah, it makes more sense for them to wait until they can afford to get a place of their own." JW wondered when he would have enough money for him and Beth to get married. "Could be some time before either of us can afford it."

"When the time is right, JW. When the time is right."

Chapter 32

Patty and Donnie looked at JW like he was speaking a new language. Mickey and a few of the older boys were listening too, but Mickey was grinning. He'd been hearing what JW thought for quite some time.

"We can't just keep letting them talk down to us, or they'll never stop," JW said, referring to the miners who shouted at the trapper boys. "We have to stick together. If we take a stand, maybe the mine owners will treat us better too."

The meeting lasted only a short while, but JW believed it was important to share what he knew with the others. He wanted them to stand up for their rights, and said that he'd arrange another meeting soon.

"What do you think?" JW asked Mickey as the other boys left.

"JB'll never be dead long as you're around," Mickey answered. "Little Donnie didn't seem to know what to think. He kept looking from you, to Patty, and then to me." Mickey laughed. "A little while ago Da was saying how you were saucin' him in front of one of the trapper boys. He was mad enough to blow his top. His face got so red when he was tellin' Ma and us, that I had to leave the room before I started laughin'. He woulda killed me."

"Yeah, I don't look forward to the next time we're in the same room. He was mad enough to hit me with his shovel, just like he was gonna the last time I talked back to him," JW said.

"Oh, and he can be quick with his mitts," Mickey said. He recalled the slap he'd gotten at the beginning of the summer, when he'd asked to use the horse to haul coal with JW. That had been the last one. If it happened again, he would go and live with his grandfather.

—

Alfred looked out the shed's window at the snow blanketing the fields and thought he should check his rabbit snares. He appreciated the kindness the Donaldson family showed him, but he wanted to help out in any way he could. He turned the damper on the coal stove to a closed position. *No sense wasting the fire when I'm not here*, he thought. Beauty had full run of the barn now; she'd be warm in there. Alfred liked that she followed him around whenever he was in the shed or barn. He wondered how she and Tennyson would get along once she realized that mice and rats were possible meals for her.

He picked up his walking stick and went outside. The air was crisp but invigorating as he made his way into the woods. He saw the tracks of many rabbits and those of some birds. The accumulated snowfall was less than two inches, but for the birds it covered some of their precious food. Several of his traps had captured rabbits.

He heard a chuffing growl as he neared one of the snares. He had surprised a lynx that was eating one of the trapped rabbits. The lynx raised its head and growled at him. Alfred moved quickly to his left, lost his footing and fell to the ground. He held tightly to his walking stick, keeping it between him and the lynx that was moving menacingly toward him. Alfred knew that lynx were not known for being aggressive to humans, so this lynx was either starving, sick or had young in the area.

Alfred considered his options: lie there or attempt to get up. Neither seemed great. If he remained on the ground, the lynx might see it as weakness and attack. If he tried to rise up, he would leave himself open for attack.

The growling got a little louder, and Alfred feared it was a signal that an attack was imminent. He gripped the stick tighter, hoping that one good strike would make the lynx reconsider. He felt the coldness from the snow beginning to seep into his joints, and he knew that if he was going to try to get up he'd have to do it pretty quick because his aging joints would soon start to seize up, making it even more difficult to rise. His beloved Jenean came to mind as the lynx edged ever closer. The prayer he sent up was not one of fear but of thanksgiving for what he thought of as a life well-lived. But Alfred was not giving up, he was just thinking of possible outcomes.

Suddenly, what appeared as a blur struck the lynx side on, sending it head over heels. A loud pain-filled squeal pierced the eerie quiet that had, to now, been punctuated only with the occasional growl from the lynx. Alfred watched as Gulliver dove forward, his teeth snapping at the stunned lynx. The lynx tried to stand its ground, but this time Gulliver was ready for battle. He moved from side to side as the lynx swung its claws at him. When the lynx swiped at him again, just missing him, Gulliver grabbed one of its back legs. A loud howl escaped the lynx's throat as it struggled free from Gulliver's grasp. It sprang to the side, making a dash for freedom with Gulliver in pursuit. Once Gulliver was convinced the lynx had no plans to stop, he hurried back to where Alfred lay.

"Good boy, good, good boy. Thank you, Gullie. You saved me," Alfred said, petting Gulliver's head.

Gulliver wagged his tail, quite proud that he was on the winning end of this most recent encounter with a lynx. The scar on his snout from his previous run-in had taught him a lesson, and he'd been prepared this time. The only blood on the ground was from the lynx and the rabbit it had been eating. Gulliver stood next to Alfred as he struggled to his feet.

Although he was in pain, Alfred collected the four rabbits from the snares and reset the wires. He checked on the other half dozen snares to make sure they hadn't been moved out of place. He leaned heavily on the walking stick and carried the rabbits in his free hand. Alfred's limp was more pronounced for the first few hundred feet, but as his muscles loosened up, he went back to his usual gait. Gulliver stayed at his side and kept watch. Alfred doubted the lynx would return anytime soon, but he'd learned a lesson today. From now on he would carry a weapon.

Chapter 33

JW and Beth spent the day looking at the new stock the Co-operative had brought in for the Christmas season. JW thought he'd seen some of the same goods last year. Perhaps any seasonal stock not sold was packed away from year to year. He was glad he'd already picked up his mother's and Beth's gifts. He hoped his mother would like the scarf he'd gotten her, and he was glad she had helped him pick out the locket for Beth. His father had told him not to waste his money on anything for him, but JW planned to get something for both him and Alfred. The little money he'd saved was quickly depleting, and he still wanted to get Beth's mother a gift. He could see a little frustration on Beth's face as she picked up the various items.

"I'm sure the prices go up every Christmas," Beth whispered.

"Do you think?" JW asked.

"Sure seems like it, JW. Well, I'm through looking."

"I thought you had to get your mother's gift today," JW said. As soon as the words left his mouth, JW realized what the problem might be.

Sure enough, Beth stood on her toes and whispered in his ear. "I don't have quite enough saved yet."

"I could give you some ... or lend you it."

Beth's eyes lit up. "Okay, if you can lend me a dollar, I will pay you back as soon as I can."

JW walked behind a bin, filled to overflowing with clothing items, and pulled some change from his pocket. He counted out the dollar and slipped it into Beth's hand. "If we have time, I'd like to take a walk up through the avenues to look out at the harbour, once we're done here."

"Sure," Beth said. Although she got to see the harbour everyday on her way to and from the hospital, she knew how much JW loved the water.

Standing on a hill overlooking the harbour, JW pointed out Davey's house. It was huge. It seemed unreasonable to JW that a family of three would live in a house better suited for ten or more people. The two large chimneys billowed black smoke into the crisp air, and JW wondered how many tons of coal was used to heat the house.

He hadn't mentioned to Beth that he'd seen Davey trudging down Pond Street to the train station with a suitcase in his hand. Although Davey had changed for the worse over the past year, JW remembered when the two of them had been friends of a sort. He knew Davey's father was a manager and perhaps part owner of the mine and that lower class and upper class seldom mixed. JW had been taught that "the love of money was the root of all evil." He wondered if just liking it a lot was sinful; it sure seemed to help things go a lot smoother when he had some.

—

"The library will be closing in about ten minutes. If anyone has any books they would like to sign out, please bring them to the desk," Mrs. Johnson said.

JW watched the few library visitors walk to the desk to sign out their books. Mrs. Johnson wished them goodnight as she locked the door behind them. The small group gathered with JW included Patty, Donnie and two of the other trap boys. JW knew Mickey would've been there if he hadn't been working. He was glad Mrs. Johnson had agreed to let him use the library for their meeting.

There was a loud knock on the door. Mrs. Johnson opened it, and Smitty and JB McLachlan entered the library. Everyone stared at JB. He was a local legend. He took the seat next to JW at the head of the table. Moments later he stood up.

"Good evening, boys. When JW said he was going to have a meeting, I asked to come and speak to you. I know some of you have only been in the mine a few months and some longer than that, but it's never too soon to learn that you have to stand up for your rights. You can't let mine owners, like Wolvin and McClurg in the recent past, nor the ones today, talk about rolling back your wages. If you let them take back what you've already earned with your blood, sweat and tears, where would they stop?" JB looked around the table, catching each person's eye until the head nodded in affirmation.

JW noticed that even Mrs. Johnson was caught up in JB's impassioned speech, nodding her head along with the boys. He wondered what he could add as JB turned the floor over to him. He took a deep breath and waited several seconds before he began.

"I'd like to thank JB for coming tonight and pointing out the importance of fighting for our rights and standing up to the mine owners. But that also brings to mind that we have to get the older miners to start respecting us as workers too. If we keep letting them talk down to us, when will it stop? When we're twenty, twenty-five?" The boys' heads were all nodding, as were Smitty's and JB's. JW caught Mrs. Johnson looking at him, smiling, and he smiled back.

Chapter 34

JW saw a group of boys gathered near the breakers. Patty seemed to be in a heated debate with several of the boys from the breakers and others who worked in the mines, and even Donnie had something to say. JW headed toward the boys but saw Mickey hurrying inside and realized he barely had time to get dressed for his shift. *I'll check with Patty later*, JW thought. As the door closed behind him, it blocked out the last rays of sunshine he'd see for the next eight hours.

"Open the door, boy."

Patty looked at the miner. "I'm having my lunch, and my name's not boy."

Shawn McGuire's puzzled look quickly turned to one of anger. "Open the door, boy, or I'll hit ya with the shovel."

Patty didn't have a father that Shawn was afraid of, and he was alone with an angry man twice his size, so he didn't know what his next move should be. He heard the squeal of wheels from a second horse-drawn tram and was relieved to see it was Smitty coming his way. Patty watched Shawn McGuire lower the shovel back on the tram. Patty walked slowly to the door and pulled the rope, opening the trap. Shawn's menacing look didn't seem as scary as before, but Patty knew he'd have to be watchful, 'cause Shawn would be at his door two or three more times this shift, and there might not be anyone else show up next time.

"What was that all about?" Smitty asked, once Shawn McGuire's tram cleared the trap door.

"I told him I was eating my lunch when he told me to open the door. And I told him my name isn't boy," Patty said.

"Does JW know about this?" Smitty asked.

"No, but me and Donnie decided we'd do our part," Patty said.

"Is Donnie working tonight?"

"Yeah, he's on the next door. Why?"

"Open the door, Patty. I wanna get there before Shawn."

Patty realized Donnie could be in danger and quickly opened the door. Smitty rushed along the tracks, pushing the small horse harder than he liked.

—

JW walked down the stairs and joined his parents for supper. The dining room table had a veritable feast on it, and he wondered if he'd missed an event. A large deer roast lay on a platter, and potatoes, turnips, carrots and corn were in bowls, as was some beautiful dark gravy that would soon smother his potatoes. He noted the fourth place setting and heard the back door open, announcing the arrival of Alfred, who sometimes joined them for an evening meal. Although he slept in the house overnight, he still liked to take most meals out in the shed.

"Alfred's nephew brought a huge buck, so you can thank him and Alfred for the feast," Mary said.

"You're welcome," Alfred said, before JW had a chance to say anything. "Please remind me to bring some meat to Gullie for saving my life."

Once grace had been said, JW began in earnest, piling food on his plate. His only complaint was that the plate was too small, and he said so, eliciting laughter from all present.

"I see you've got the boys stirred up," Andrew said.

JW laid his fork down and continued chewing for a moment. "What do you mean, Da?"

"Patty and Donnie not opening the doors quickly enough, and the boys at the breakers have been letting quite a few rocks get by them."

"I didn't tell them—" JW stopped in mid-sentence, remembering his words from the meeting. Although he didn't want them to act badly, he was sure they only heard his passionate plea for them to stand up for themselves. "I only meant they had rights. I didn't want them to be insubordinate or put themselves in danger."

"I'm not saying standing up for yourself is wrong," Andrew said. "I've done a bit of it myself. I just think it best you figure out a better way for them to get their point across. If this news gets to the bosses, there's nothing I can do to save their jobs. It cost poor Donnie."

"What do you mean?"

"Patty and Donnie chose to talk back to McGuire, and he hit Donnie with a shovel."

JW stared at his father.

"The same might have happened to Patty if Smitty hadn't arrived in time. Smitty said by the time he got to Donnie's door, Shawn was already through, and Donnie was holding his arm. It's not broken, but it's got a gash on it and is badly bruised."

"I never meant for them to stand up to McGuire on their own. What's gonna happen to Mr. McGuire?"

"Nothin'. Donnie's too afraid to say anything. You better keep a watchful eye. I'm sure he blames you."

For the first time in recent memory, JW's head over-rode his stomach, and he pushed his plate to the middle of the table, wondering how he could fix this. He wished he'd thought to warn the boys to be respectful. The saying, "the pen is mightier than the sword" came to mind, and JW knew he'd have to call another meeting right away. He reasoned that if his words had incited bad behaviour, his message had failed. He thought a discussion with JB was in order.

—

"I've more to say, but I'm going to turn the floor over to JW Donaldson," JB McLachlan said.

The room went silent when JW stood where JB had been. He saw the look of curiosity on some of the men and indifference on others, but the best was the sneer on Shawn McGuire's face. JW began haltingly but quickly found his voice when the sneer grew bigger on McGuire's face.

"I've been talking with JB for years and thought I un-derstood what he meant about us and them, but it wasn't until I was on the cage where two men died, and me and Mickey thought we were going to die too, that the point was driven home. Or I should say, shortly after. When we got to the surface one of the managers was only concerned about getting production moving again. I heard him shouting, 'Clean up the mess and get back to work. We've got orders to fill.' He didn't mention the loss of two men, two good men, who wouldn't get to go home to their families again, or the fact that their families had no one to care for them."

Most of the men gathered seemed to be listening, thinking about their lost friends, as JW continued.

"I read some stuff about indentured servants, which was pretty much what mining families were turned into by the company stores, a place to run up bills until the company kept everything you earned. The owners still treat us like we're paying off a debt, instead of treating us as valuable, skilled employees."

"Well, some of us are skilled. Others are still wet behind the ears and afraid of the dark, or have daddies to care for them," Shawn McGuire said, eliciting a few chuckles from the men.

JW stared at Shawn. "Isn't that what a father is supposed to do?"

"Anyway," he continued, "most of the trapper boys and those leading trams said they don't mind the work. They said the worst part of the job is the few ... the few older miners who are mean to them, hollering for no reason. One even hit a young fellow with a shovel. Now that's pretty cowardly. As for fear, I recently heard there are miners who won't go down in the cage, because they're afraid the cable might break. Guess they're not the real miners, the trapper boys are, 'cause they're leaving the doors and going down there."

JW turned to JB. "I just have a few more things to say and then I'll give the floor back to JB. The reason I wanted to talk tonight is that I've been meeting with the young people and telling them about unity and how the union works together for the rights of all men, and boys too. They come to the meetings with questions about the few who holler at them. Some of them are scared, and when they're hollered at too, it's pretty hard to convince them of the importance of us all sticking together."

A chair scraped loudly, and JW watched Shawn Mc-Guire get ready to grandstand.

"I didn't come here to listen to no boy tell me how I should act," Shawn said.

"If we can't treat each other right, how can we expect to be treated right by management?" JW said, then added, "A house divided cannot stand."

JW nodded to JB, who got quickly to his feet.

"Lots to consider. Thank you, JW. See you again," JB said, signalling it was time for him to leave the meeting.

Chapter 35

The next evening, JW was back in the library looking at the shelves filled with books. He remembered, fondly, many of the ones he'd read over the years and how the stories had taken him to places he supposed he'd never get to see.

"JW?"

He looked up at Mrs. Johnson.

"I was quite impressed by what you had to say the other night, and it seemed so was everyone else in the room. Patty and Donnie and the other boys were paying close attention, listening to your every word. I don't know what your plans are, but I think you should consider this," she said, laying a piece of paper on the table in front of him. "Grade eleven is a junior matriculation and what you need to go to Provincial Normal College in Truro. In one year, you'd be a teacher."

"In a year? A teacher? Like you? Thanks very much, Mrs. Johnson. I'll look it over."

The door opened and several people came in the library. JW saw that Mrs. Johnson wanted to say more, but he knew she had to see to the new arrivals.

As if reading his thoughts, Mrs. Johnson turned and said, "Oh, and JW, the tuition is little or nothing at all. You just need a place to stay and money for food."

"Thanks again," JW said, and folded the paper and put it in his pocket. He knew she'd be busy for a while, so he would check back later. He waved to her as he left. *A teacher, I could be a teacher*, JW thought. *In a year, I could be a teacher*.

The walk through town put JW in a festive mood. Decorations adorned the storefronts, and passersby said, "Merry Christmas," putting aside, for a moment, the worries of everyday life. JW thought of Charles Dickens's novella, A Christmas Carol, and knew that for many it would be a difficult time. Although Roy Wolvin had left a few years ago, the former president of the British Empire Steel Corporation – BESCO – the company that operated the mine, was still referred to as Roy the Wolf and fit the character of Scrooge perfectly. Roy the Wolf had surely played a role in trying to decrease the surplus population by starving out the miners and their families, and like Scrooge had rolled back the wages of his workers. Unlike Scrooge, he didn't transform into a caring, loving person. He just left.

JW put that out of his mind as he saw a little girl looking in the Co-operative window at the toys displayed. The squeals of glee brought a smile to his face.

"Well, hello, JW."

At the sound of Beth's voice, his smile increased. "I thought you were at the hospital today, Beth. Don't you have exams?"

"Yes, on Monday, the day before Christmas Eve. They let us out early today, and Sally and I came in to look around. I've been studying all week, so I needed a break. I could spare an hour later, if you're not working tonight."

"I'm off until Monday. I could help you study later."

"Why not come over after supper, and we'll go for a walk? I plan to study again tonight and all day tomorrow."

"I'll be there. I'd like to talk to you about some things. See you then."

Beth leaned in and gave his hand a squeeze.

JW decided to head home to finish any chores so he'd be ready after supper to go to Beth's. November had been cold and quite a bit of snow had fallen, but it had turned rainy and unseasonably warm for the past week, even though it was almost Christmas. JW noticed bare patches of earth here and there on the sides of the road. He hoped the weather would not be too harsh this winter and there'd be an early spring. Drift ice usually took a while to leave, but once that was gone, if he had the boat finished, he'd test it out on the water. He had discussed naming the boat with Beth, and she said she was honoured that he considered putting her name on his boat.

"Of course your mother's name should go first. Besides," she'd continued, "the *Mary Beth* flows better."

JW had been relieved when Beth had said that, and he'd smiled when his mother had said he should give his boat Beth's full name. The *Mary Elizabeth* was the name he chose, named after both of them. He put his hand in his pocket and felt the folded paper Mrs. Johnson had given him. He'd never considered that he had enough education to go to college. A few months ago, JW believed he was stuck in the coal mines for the rest of his working life, but now the world once again seemed a whole lot bigger. He had options: Teacher's College, use his boat for fishing or moving supplies, or stay in the coal mines. JW's mind was spinning. He had a lot to think about, but he was looking forward to the future for the first time since starting in the mine last summer.

The tapping of Gulliver's cold wet nose against his hand pushed the thoughts away. JW bent down and petted Gullie's head and back. He was glad Gulliver was still quite young. Poor Lightning and Tennyson were both starting to show their age.

So is Alfred, JW thought. It was better Alfred had moved into a bedroom in the house, at least for the nights. He'd worried he would stay in the shed instead. JW had grown very fond of the old man. It was like having another grandfather. JW hadn't thought that he might be like the son or grandson that Alfred had never had. They got along so well, and each tried to lighten the other's tasks.

The house and barn came into view, and JW started off at a slow jog, his satchel tapping against his side. Gulliver fell into rhythm beside him. JW had wood and coal to get in, and he was sure there'd be some other stuff that needed doing. He saw Alfred standing outside, leaning against the barn, as if he was waiting for him. He waved to him, and Alfred returned it and made his way toward the house.

"The coal and wood are in and the stalls are cleaned out. Are you ready to do some work on the boat later?" Alfred asked.

"I'm sorry, I forgot we had plans. Beth asked me to come over for an hour after supper."

Alfred smiled. "That is where I would be going, if I were your age. Perhaps when you get back. I will have a nap after supper and be ready when you return. We can get a few pieces on the hull tonight."

"That would be great. Thank you. And thanks for doing the chores."

JW held the door for Alfred and followed him into the house. The aroma of supper wafting through the doorway started JW's stomach growling. All other thoughts left his mind as he watched his mother dip up his meal.

—

The hour with Beth turned to two, and their talk of possible future plans had consumed the evening. The moon was bright in the sky as JW walked homeward. It was later than he'd planned, and he didn't have the heart to wake Alfred when he arrived home.

Chapter 36

Mickey walked ahead. JW had to bend his knees to keep from hitting his head.

"These tunnels are some low, Mick."

"You're spoiled from loading the trams. Tonight we get to work in the three footers – picks and shovels."

"I'd have to lie on my stomach to get that low," JW said, then laughed.

"You wouldn't be the first – or last," Mickey said.

The deeper they went, the staler the air got. JW felt his chest rise as he worked to get more air into his lungs. A feeling of panic washed over him, and he wondered if the trapper boy had fallen asleep with the trap door open, letting all the fresh air escape.

"Hey, Mick, you having trouble breathing?"

"Yeah, it's normal. The deeper we go, the less air. Don't breathe deep. Just breathe normal. You'll get used to it."

JW hoped he wouldn't have to get used to breathing stale air. "I was worried the trap was left open, and we'd become the ghosts that haunt the trapper boys."

Mickey stopped. "Well, there she is, JW."

JW looked at the hole in the wall in front of them. It didn't look like much of a tunnel. There wouldn't be enough room to get a full swing of the pick, and they'd have to work on their knees. The floor was covered with coal and other rubble. JW pushed some away to make a smooth area to kneel down.

Gripping the pick handle in the middle, JW swung against the side of the tunnel. Pieces of coal splintered and flew directly into his face, stinging. He watched Mickey swing, and more coal fell.

"Don't we have to worry about a cave-in?" JW asked.

"When we get in a little deeper, we have to put in some posts to secure the ceiling."

"So this is gonna be slow going."

"Listen. What's that?" Mickey said.

JW and Mickey turned toward the sound of someone coming up the tunnel. The bobbing light soon showed it was Anderson. He'd gone back to the mine in New Waterford or Glace Bay, so they hadn't expected to see him.

"Tunnel's not deep enough. Gonna hafta do some more blasting to get her deeper."

That was more words than JW had ever heard Anderson say.

"Donaldson, you place the charge."

"I can do it, Anderson," Mickey said. "I've done it before."

"No, Donaldson gets a turn tonight. He ain't ever gonna learn if he don't do one."

"No one said they'd be blasting tonight," Mickey said.

"I just did," Anderson said.

JW listened to Mickey and Anderson go back and forth.

"If it's got to be done, I'll do it," JW said. "Just show me what to do."

JW placed the black powder in the hole Mickey had drilled and set the fuse exactly as Anderson had shown him. He scurried up the tunnel where Mickey and Anderson waited, expecting the blast to go off before he reached them. The seconds turned to a minute. Another minute passed.

"You'll have to go check on why it didn't blow," Anderson said.

Mickey started to say something, but JW cut him off.

"I set it the way you showed me. I'm not going to check it. If there's something wrong with it, it's because you showed me wrong."

"I'm boss down here, boy!"

"Then you should go see what's wrong!" JW said.

"I'll go, but you won't have a job here come morning."

JW didn't respond. He watched Anderson walk to the hole and followed a short distance behind. Anderson pulled at the charge, and JW was knocked off his feet by the force of the blast. Although his ears were ringing, JW heard a howling sound like an animal caught in a trap. JW saw Anderson trying to crawl toward him, then noticed his mangled hand. Fingers were missing. Blood flowed profusely. JW quickly pulled his belt from his pants and used it as a tourniquet to stop the bleeding.

Anderson was in shock and moments later passed out. Mickey hurried to his side, and he and JW decided to carry Anderson back to the cage.

—

"Two of his fingers were missing when he arrived at the hospital, and the doctor had to amputate another one three days later," Beth said. "He's been there ten days, and it seems like he'll be there a while longer. He wasn't too pleased to be in hospital over Christmas, but the doctor said it will be a slow recovery, and he's worried about possible infection. I'm not to speak about patients outside the hospital, but I know you and Mickey were the ones that got him to the cage."

"Yeah, we were," JW said.

"The doctor said the tourniquet probably saved Mr. Anderson's life. That he might have bled to death. Where'd you learn that, JW?"

"I must've read it somewhere." Then he remembered his father had told him how he'd used it on the battlefields during the Great War. Andrew had joined the Cape Breton Highlanders in 1916 and gone overseas until the war was over two years later.

"Well it's a good thing you did."

"I'm glad the doctor was able to patch him up. Anderson wanted me to check on the charge, and I wouldn't. If I had, it could be me in the hospital bed. Cave-ins and explosions and runaway trips and broken cables on cages, not to mention back-breaking work on a good day. A miner doesn't have much to look forward to. To top it all off, a boss that doesn't want to pay him decent wages for his hard work. The majority of the miners share a bond, a camaraderie, but there are some like Anderson and Shawn McGuire that can make the days and nights seem excessively long, especially for the boys. Sorry. I get worked up, thinking about it."

Beth had come to JW's to see the progress on the boat. The two of them were huddled together in the barn. The January weather had turned colder, the temperature well below freezing.

"It looks ready to sail, JW. Is it finished?" Beth wanted to give JW something more pleasant to talk about.

"Not quite, but really close. It'll be ready by the time the ice is out of the harbour."

"You must be excited," Beth said.

JW noticed that Beth hadn't responded when he'd said it could have been him in the hospital instead of Anderson. He knew she wanted him out of the pit.

"Yes, I'm pretty excited. Like I mentioned before, I was thinking that I could use it to fish or carry goods, maybe both. And ever since Mrs. Johnson said I have enough education to go to Teacher's College, I've been thinking about that a lot. In a year I'd be a teacher. Can you imagine, Beth, being able to teach young people the importance of education? Mrs. Johnson pointed out that my friends listen to me. She said that I could make a difference. Change the world, at least for some of the boys around here."

Beth smiled as JW talked about possibilities, but she knew that it was difficult to leave an actual job to go after a maybe job. Still, she hoped JW would choose teaching, or at least using his boat. In her short time at the hospital, she'd already seen miners who'd been killed, others who had been maimed and ones with lasting lung issues that stole their very breath. And the dangers were real for the new miners as well as the experienced ones.

"Sounds like you've got some choices to make, JW."

"Yeah, I guess, but that's a few months away, and I gotta work nights next week. Might get a few hours to spend with Alfred working on the boat. Can't you just picture it, riding the waves with the wind blowing in our faces?"

"Sounds wonderful. Just hope it's warmer than it is right now," Beth said, and snuggled closer to JW. He put his arm around her and drew her nearer. He could feel her shivering from the cold.

JW put his coat around Beth's shoulders then quickly cleaned the stalls and threw some fresh hay in for Lightning and the cow. Meanwhile, Beth petted Beauty. Although she was a barn cat, she acted more like a house pet, spending her nights in the shed, sleeping on the cot, perhaps missing Alfred now that he slept in the house. JW had seen her chase mice, but she seemed to leave the rats alone, perhaps in deference to Tennyson. Alfred fed her cooked rabbit and scraps from his meals. She hadn't yet gotten the taste for the mice and squirrels that also called the barn home.

JW pulled the barn door tightly behind them as he and Beth left, to keep the wind and drafts out. They waved to JW's mother, silhouetted in the kitchen window, busy with the supper preparations. Alfred and Andrew stood by the chicken coop, each with several eggs in their hands.

"Tell Ma I'll be back for supper, Da," JW said. "I'm just going to walk Beth home."

"Oh, I don't think she'd be too worried that you'd miss supper."

Beth laughed. "Not likely. I think he carries a snack in his pockets. Bye, Mr. Donaldson. Bye, Alfred."

"I am a growing boy, after all," JW said. Gulliver caught up to them and tapped his nose against Beth's hand.

"Hello, Gullie the Hero," JW said. He had been very impressed when Alfred told him how Gullie had protected him in the woods last month.

Gulliver did his usual full-body shuffle, enjoying the extra attention of late. After getting petted by both Beth and JW, he trotted alongside, keeping an eye out for any wildlife, especially a lynx.

Chapter 37

JW's headlamp illuminated the floor in front of him as he scanned the coal that had fallen from the last blast. "Look, Mick!" Large sections of the coal displayed ferns and other plant life.

"Been a while since we looked for fossils, JW," Mickey said.

The experience of the cave-in three years earlier – Mickey being trapped and JW helping to dig him and the others out – had made the boys put aside their youthful desire to search for fossils.

"Yeah, but look at how many there are, Mickey. I wonder if there are any with animals in them." For a moment, JW was transported to a time when all the world held wonder for him and Mickey.

The scraping of Mickey's shovel brought him back to the present. "Guess they're just rocks for the boys at the breakers to pick out," JW said, and joined Mickey to load the trams. The tunnel was low, and after a few hours of shovelling, JW was glad it was time to break for lunch. His back was sore from being bent over, and he supposed Mickey's was too.

He watched Mickey quickly devour two sandwiches and a cookie or two.

"I've seen seagulls eat slower than you," JW said. "Don't worry, I wasn't gonna ask you for any."

Mickey laughed. "Yeah, almost as fast as you. I learned to eat like that these past months working with you."

"I might have to give you a new nickname. Seagull."

"No thanks. Mick suits me just fine. Besides, I can think of a couple new ones for you. Hollow Leg, or, I know, Lumpy, for all the times you bumped your head on the beams."

"Deal," JW said. "No new nicknames." They shook hands.

"That's all we'd need," Mickey said. "Here comes Lumpy and Seagull."

JW and Mickey laughed, and their laughter echoed along the tunnels. Despite the hard work, JW had become aware of the camaraderie that most miners felt toward each other. Oh, there were a few hard cases, but he imagined that was the same as with most jobs. Smitty and Patty and Donnie were all good fellas, and the men he met a short time ago, Butts and Dawe, were two of the nicest men he'd ever known. They were the ones who had blasted the coal seam for him and Mickey tonight so they'd have coal to shovel.

"You know, Mick, ever since Anderson's accident I've been nervous about having to set another charge. I did everything he told me to do."

"That black powder seems to have a mind of its own. I've only used it a few times, and I've been lucky so far, but there's been more than Anderson that's been hurt, some a lot worse than him. Maybe it was wet, or maybe he didn't show you right."

"I'm not in a hurry to try again," JW said.

"Most times they get someone smaller to set the charge, 'cause they can get into smaller spots."

"Good to know," JW said. "I'll be sure to eat extra to keep growing."

"Don't think you hafta grow much more. If you do, you won't fit in any of the tunnels."

"Be nice if we worked on the surface, and I don't mean at the breakers or anywhere connected to coal." JW didn't want to sound like he was complaining and changed the subject. "How's Sally getting along in nursing?"

"Pretty good. It seems she and Beth will be all done their training come summer. I'm glad Sally decided to go back after what happened. Bad enough to see her first dead person as part of her job, but for it to be her Uncle Artie was a real shocker."

"Yeah, it must have been especially tough for her. It was scary enough for us seeing them like that. I still think about Artie and Gerry every time I step in the cage. Bad enough we have to drop like a rock off a cliff for almost a thousand feet, but we have to worry that the cable's gonna break too."

"If the cage hadn't gotten wedged against the shaft, we'd all be angels."

JW and Mickey looked at each other and took a deep breath. The pause was interrupted by a familiar noise. Several rats had smelled the food and gathered nearby for any crumbs. The boys threw the crusts up the tunnel and listened to the squealing sounds as the rats raced toward their feast.

—

JW and Beth sat in the town library. Several books lay on the table in front of them.

JW whispered, "Mrs. Johnson sent a letter of reference with my application to Teacher's College."

Beth's eyes glistened. She was happy he'd made up his mind to apply. "What did she say?"

They heard someone clear their throat behind them and turned to see Mrs. Johnson, who was smiling.

"I wrote that JW had been one of the best students I'd ever had the pleasure to teach, and that if he wanted, he could be a doctor, lawyer or whatever he wished. I then added who better to teach young minds of tomorrow than someone who had excelled in school, someone who could impress upon young minds the importance of education."

Mrs. Johnson smiled again then headed back to her desk. She stopped. "Oh, Beth, I would have written the same letter for you, had you decided to become a teacher. But I know you'll be a wonderful nurse."

"Thank you, Mrs. Johnson," Beth and JW said in unison. They looked at each other and laughed.

"We better get on our way, Beth," JW said. "I haven't told Ma and Da about applying. I was going to wait until I heard back from the college, because I might not get in, but I think I should tell them tonight, before someone else does."

"Oh, you'll get in, I'm sure, but it's best you tell them that you applied," Beth said.

Chapter 38

JW's mother and father were seated at the dining room table having tea when he arrived home. Since JW's first time in the pit, three years ago, the dining room had become used more often. It was no longer only for special occasions. JW poured a cup of tea for himself and joined his parents.

"Just got back from Beth's. Her Ma said to say hi. Where's Alfred?"

"Out checking on the boat. He must circle it fifty times a day looking for flaws," Andrew said, smiling at his son.

"It looks beautiful, JW," his mother said. "You must be so pleased."

"I really am, Ma. From a raft with a canvas sail last summer to a real boat this summer. I never thought I'd get to own one, let alone help build it. Couldn't have done it without all the help, first with Alfred teaching me, and then Da making the tools and showing me how to make them. Smitty and Mickey coming over on their days off. Even Patty and Donnie helped." JW smiled.

Andrew and Mary looked at their son and couldn't help smiling along with him.

"You know, Beth will be a nurse come summer, and she and I were talking." JW saw an expectant look on his parents' faces and realized what they were thinking. "No, we're not getting married. We are, but not really soon. Still don't think she can cook like you yet, Ma," JW said, and they all laughed.

"What were you talkin' about?" his father asked.

"Well, she's gonna be a nurse by summer," JW repeated. "And Mrs. Johnson said I have enough education to apply to be a teacher, which I could be by the following summer, so I'm thinking about, come fall, going to Teacher's College."

JW expected a look of relief from his mother but really wasn't surprised to see one on his father's face as well. They had narrowly escaped death in the cage. He waited while his parents digested the news. His mother was first to speak.

"You've always made good choices since you were a little boy, and not always the easiest ones. I think you're making another good one."

Before JW could respond, his father added.

"Your mother's right, JW. Oh, you could be a fine miner and eke out a living the same way I have and many other miners have, but I like that you're going to try something else. So what happens in the fall? I mean ... what's it gonna cost?"

"Mrs. Johnson said the tuition is little or nothing, that I'd just need a place to stay and money for food," JW said.

"Oh, that's a deal breaker," his mother said.

JW looked at his parents, then smiled with relief when they broke into laughter.

"We could never afford to feed you if you leave home," Mary Donaldson said, still chuckling.

"I might have to take you with me, Ma. Da and Alfred can look after themselves."

"You're on your own, son," Andrew said. "But I do have a cousin or two living in Truro, and I'm sure one of them would take you in. Earl's got a small farm and is getting on in age. I'm sure you'd earn your keep by helping out," his father said.

The reality of the situation was setting in, and JW realized he'd be away from everyone he loved, or who loved him, for nine months. All the work looking after Lightning and the cow and the chickens would fall to his parents. He'd never been away from home for longer than a night, and that was just a sleepover in the fort, or at Mickey's when he'd been much younger. He'd been close enough to home that he could walk there in half an hour.

The sense of adventure pushed away the anxiety of being away from home. He hoped Alfred would stay, and it seemed likely that he would. He would be a help with some of the chores that JW usually did. JW's mind continued to race as he considered what his parents had said about his decision. He knew they were both proud of him, but it was nice to hear it. He hoped he would get accepted into college for the fall, and he would do his best to continue to make them proud of him.

JW stood back and took in the finished boat – his boat. It was beautiful, but he knew the real test was a couple of months away when it would be launched. That would determine if it was seaworthy. The smile on Alfred's face told JW that it was likely it would be.

JW had watched in awe as Alfred's skilled hands chiselled Mary Elizabeth across the hull of the boat. The dark red colouring he used on the lettering was a present from Alfred's nephew, Daniel. It stained the wood, and Alfred had added a shellac finish to ensure the salt water would not wash it away.

JW hadn't forgotten that he had to cut wood for the mill as payment for the lumber the owner had provided for his boat, but he had pushed it to the back of his mind. He knew it would take a few weeks to cut and deliver the wood. Thankfully, Alfred had told him he would mark the trees he should cut. Alfred had provided almost everything JW needed for the boat, except for the hardware and pulleys. JW's father made them to Alfred's specifications. The only thing missing had been the sails. To JW's surprise, Beth's father had arrived at the barn last week; he had salvaged old sails from a shipbuilding project that could be cut and hemmed to fit the Mary Elizabeth.

JW had been planning to just have Beth, Alfred and his parents on the original launch but had quickly revised his list to include Smitty and Mickey, as well as Beth's parents and sister. He'd added Sally and Patty to the list, and then remembered Donnie. The boat was going to be pretty much filled to capacity if everyone invited showed up.

JW hoped he would be in Teacher's College come September, but that gave him the spring and summer to spend on the lake, sailing and fishing. JW knew being a teacher would give him the best of both worlds, steady work and additional free time in the summers.

As Alfred and JW walked toward the house, JW thought about the impact that Alfred had had on him, from Alfred's first night, just trying to get out of the cold, to becoming part of the family.

JB McLachlan's words also came to mind. JW couldn't quote them precisely, but he had taken from them that not all of life's lessons are taught in books and schools, and that the true heroes are the working men and women. JW decided he would be sure to tell his future students what JB had to say. But for now, he planned to continue to meet with

Mickey, Patty and Donnie and any other young miners to try to come up with ways to make the coal mine a better, safer place to work.

In the distance, JW saw a piece of land overlooking the water and thought it would be a nice place to build a house. The skills he'd learned while building the boat would come in handy when the time came for him and Beth to build a home. But that was in the future.

Chapter 39

"How do you like teaching, so far?" Beth asked. She was excited for JW and very happy that he was back home. She had missed him so much the nine months he'd been away at Teacher's College.

The past three-and-a-half months they had seen each other more than they had in the previous two years – they had been practically inseparable. The Mary Elizabeth had been put to good use exploring the inlets and coves up and down St. Andrew's Channel. All summer long, Beth saw an excitement in JW as he captained his ship. She knew it was a boat, but when his hand rested on the tiller, she knew his mind had him in a sailing ship, off on an adventure in a far-away land. He still had a deep tan from the summer spent on the boat. Hers was beginning to fade, but she'd only spent days off on the boat. He and Alfred, Smitty and Mickey had done a fair bit of fishing. The winter months' meals would consist of a lot of salted and smoked fish, both cod and mackerel.

JW took a moment to collect his thoughts before answering. "I'm really glad to be teaching, but seeing some of those little boys coming to school with cut and broken fingers is difficult. Some are so tired, they should be home in their beds, and others are only a few years younger than you and me. I've decided to take an active role and meet with the miners, young and old, mostly the young ones, to try to get them to learn about their rights and how to lobby for better working conditions."

"I know," said Beth. "I often see these little ones, who should be playing games, waiting on a chair to be patched up so they can go back to work."

"I have boys in the class who've already repeated the grade twice. They're smart enough to do the lessons, but the shiftwork means they miss as much school as they attend." JW looked at Beth. "I spoke to Mrs. Johnson about setting up night school classes for the children, and she thought it was a great idea. She said we should open it up to adults as well."

"Sounds like she plans to be part of it," Beth said

JW nodded.

"Do you think adults would even consider doing that? Going to school, I mean?" Beth asked.

"Don't know, but I do know there are some in the mines who never got a chance to go to school much past second or third grade, which means little or no chance of promotion, at least not one where you have to read and write."

"Wouldn't it be wonderful if some did come to the night school classes?" Beth said. "Knowledge is power."

"What?' JW said.

"You remember. Mrs. Johnson told us that in grade eight, that the more you knew—"

"I remember. That's what I'll use to try and encourage them to come to class. My main focus is the children, but I hope both come. Thanks, Beth," JW said, and kissed her.

—

JW looked at the children seated before him. His conversation with Beth last week about how knowledge is power stuck with him, and he thought the more power he could bring to the boys and girls, the better. He remembered the times spent in class with Beth. How they were often first and second in the running for prizes for English or French. His mind drifted back to grade eight when he and Beth were both awarded prizes for English – a set of books, the classics. He looked at the children before him and at those same books, which were lying on his desk. The Count of Monte Cristo, which brought to mind the darkened tunnels, and Moby Dick, which made him think of the majesty of the ocean and the creatures therein. His eyes lingered on Robinson Crusoe, and he wondered if the content might be too much for some of the children, as parts of it troubled him. He looked at the novel Little Women, which both Beth and Mrs. Johnson said would be well received by the young ladies in the classroom. He hoped he could convince the children to read simply for the pleasure it could bring them. He knew reading would instill a sense of adventure in them, dreams and aspirations for a better life.

JW sensed that most of the class were distracted by something in the corner to his left where he'd set up a small table with rocks and coal, both of which had fossils encased within them. He realized that they were staring at the blackboard, not the table. He guessed someone might have drawn a picture or written something on the board.

When he turned to look, he discovered the blackboard was as clean as the previous class had left it. The children were staring at the foot-and-a-half piece of leather that resembled a beaver's tail and hung from a nail beside the blackboard. He knew the strap was widely used for various infractions, real or imagined. He remembered getting the strap a few times over the years. Some were for being late back from recess and some were because the teacher couldn't figure out who had thrown the piece of chalk or eraser, so all the boys in the vicinity got it. JW wondered whether, sometimes, it was wielded just because the teacher was in a bad mood.

The walls were thin between the classrooms, and he felt himself cringe whenever he heard the loud crack of the strap, like a whip being snapped in the air, followed by the muffled cries of the child who'd received it. Once he'd counted ten cracks in succession and wondered what terrible crime had been committed.

JW rose from his chair, pulled the strap from the nail and threw it on his desk. Using his thumb and forefinger, he wiggled the nail back and forth, pulling it from the wall. He opened the top drawer of his desk, pushed the strap to the back of it and threw the nail in the waste bin. He would have liked to have thrown the strap in the bin as well but knew it wasn't his place to do so. He hoped it would stay hidden – and unused – at least for a while.

He thought of grade eight again, the year he'd spent in Mrs. Johnson's class. Never once throughout the year did she ever use or threaten to use the strap. JW hoped he would never have to use it, because the lesson he'd learned that year from her was that fear was not a good motivator.

JW was happy to see the children's eyes were now drawn to the fossils, and he began his lesson, telling them when and where he'd found them, pointing out that some of the students in the class had seen them first-hand underground.

—

Standing on the hilltop overlooking the mine, JW felt Beth's hand slip into his. He had missed her so much during the time spent at Teacher's College. They watched as the shift changed, men and boys squinting as their eyes tried to adjust to the sunlight after a night spent underground.

"Are you getting used to the children calling you Mr. Donaldson?" Beth asked.

"Not really, Nurse Jessome. Maybe in a few months," JW said. "Let's hope I can keep some of them out of the mines and that those I can't don't end up with you, needing to be patched up."

Beth looked into JW's eyes and gave a sad smile. They both knew that change came slowly and that for the foreseeable future, boys would continue to enter the mines, and many would be seen by her, and others, to be patched up.

They walked back toward the Donaldsons' farm. It was time to pick out a piece of land, time to build a house, time to see what the future would bring.

The End

Acknowledgements

My sincere thanks to Cape Breton University Press and to Mike Hunter, Editor-in-Chief. Thank you to Marianne Ward for her wonderful editorial suggestions.

I would also like to thank the following people for their assistance: The underground guides at the Miner's Museum, and Michael G. MacDonald, who is always available to read a first draft. Thank you to all who read *Trapper Boy* and offered words of encouragement. Thanks again to all the boys, girls and men who toiled underground and the women who awaited their return.

Most of all, thank you to Joanne for her continued love and support, and for reading everything I write.

H.R.M.

Hugh R. MacDonald is a writer of fiction, and a singer/songwriter, whose work has been in a number of anthologies, and online. Hugh has been a member of the Writers Union of Canada and the Writers Federation of Nova Scotia (WFNS) for many years. His YA novel, *Trapper Boy* was published by Cape Breton University Press – *Us & Them* is the sequel.

Hugh's song, "Trapper Boy," which he wrote prior to the novel of the same name, has been added to the repertoire of the world famous Men of the Deeps Coal Miners' Chorus, and was included on their 50th anniversary compilation CD, *Coal to Gold* (2016). Hugh's original song "A Cape Breton Lament" was included on the CD *Cape Breton Songs of Steel, Coal and Protest*, produced by Dr. Richard MacKinnon (Cape Breton University).

Trapper Boy was selected by Dr. Patrick Howard of Cape Breton University's Education Department as a novel around which to develop a Teacher Resource. The resource is currently available at no charge for teachers using Trapper Boy.

Hugh is a member of the Writers in the Schools (WITS) program through WFNS. Hugh enjoys going into schools to meet with young people and sharing his passion for writing. His presentation includes readings from his work, using his songs and his videos to share thoughts on his writing process, and encouraging young people to try their own hand at writing. WITS grade level P-12. Trapper Boy was included in The Canadian Children's Book Centre's Best Books for Kids and Teens Spring Edition 2013.

Hugh is a graduate of Cape Breton University, and works in the human service field.